THE WOMAN IN MY HOME

DIANA WILKINSON

Boldwood

First published in Great Britain in 2023 by Boldwood Books Ltd.

Cover Design by Head Design Ltd.

Cover Photography: Shutterstock

A CIP catalogue record for this book is available from the British Library.

Paperback ISBN 978-1-83751-029-0

Large Print ISBN 978-1-83751-028-3

Hardback ISBN 978-1-83751-027-6

Ebook ISBN 978-1-83751-030-6

Kindle ISBN 978-1-83751-031-3

Audio CD ISBN 978-1-83751-022-1

MP3 CD ISBN 978-1-83751-023-8

Digital audio download ISBN 978-1-83751-025-2

Boldwood Books Ltd
23 Bowerdean Street
London SW6 3TN
www.boldwoodbooks.com

To Mum and Dad.
And to Ballyholme... a tiny corner of heaven.

Before you embark on a journey of revenge,
dig two graves.

— CONFUCIUS

THE PLOT

It's 11 p.m. Pitch black. An owl hoots, a sarcastic scream of company. The squawk makes me freeze. I think of Squid Games. *One, two, three red lights. If I move, I'll be shot. A salvo of bullets that'll blow my brains out.*

It's that crazy what I'm about to do. Not to mention what I've already done. I deserve to be shot, but not without a fight. I feel delirious, hysterical. Adrenaline, fear, and anticipation are a heady cocktail.

I unwind the metal tape measure till it stretches to just over six feet. It should be ample. I dig the heel of my shoe in at each end of the designated plot, then repeat for the width. A generous four feet. The tape measure doesn't lock, recoils across my fingers, and gashes a bloodied line across the inside of my palm. Shit. Shit. Shit.

The owl hoots again. Yoo-hoo. I see you. *The hoot sounds like a laugh, but that's no surprise. The scene is comical. Even to me, but needs must. I didn't discuss the details of my plan, suffice though that I shared the intent. Well, it was my intent to share, without voicing the details. Who does share murder stories anyway? Certainly not personal ones. I hoot back at the owl.*

There is plenty of choice when trying to decide on how to dispose of a body. You'd be surprised. I googled all the options, which I now run through in my head. Like a final summing up, as I convince the jury I've made the right decision.

I pace up and down, across the plot, and stride over the diagonals. Perhaps dumped at sea would have been better. But there's always CCTV cameras, randomly positioned along arterial roads. Even country lanes aren't safe, random beasts roaming into headlights, causing carnage. Creating a staged abduction in the park. Any park. Which park though? Google wasn't as helpful as I'd hoped. Then there is the close to home disposal.

Even with my relatively strong arms, I'm not sure I could have moved a body any real distance without some help. As it is, humping it into a car would have been a nightmare. As soon as the deed was done, I managed to drag the leaden weight down the stairs. I then hoisted the still warm cadaver, with not some little effort, onto the wheeled palette on which the wooden planks had been stacked. I'd lifted the planks off earlier, in preparation.

All that's left to do is wheel the palette a couple of feet, roll the body over until it tumbles into the grave. It's pretty goddam smart to be honest.

I walk backwards, forwards, sideways, around, and back again before I finally pick up the spade. And begin to dig.

Two hours in. I've hardly scraped the surface. Shit. Shit. Shit. The earth is summer baked, solid, and only starts to loosen when I unravel the hose by the fence, and spend a good ten minutes soaking the surface. I finally make progress, the hole becoming more of a pit, and I dare to breathe again.

Three hours in. Sweat drips off me like water from a leaky pipe. It coats my vision, the torch on my mobile phone flickering in and out as I try to blink back the focus.

Four hours in. I set the spade down, and walk once more around the plot. It's taking shape. At last I'm hopeful I can pull it off.

I knock back another bottle of water, the liquid refluxing when it hits the back of my throat, and pick up the spade.

Five hours. I feel like a prisoner working for the Nazis, every weakened effort getting another lash.

Until it's finally done. 4.28 a.m.

I move across to the palette and the roughly packaged body. The black bin bags have rips, gaps, and I gag when frozen flesh appears. But I concentrate on pushing the contraption up the garden, the wheels stubborn on the uneven path slabs, inch by sweaty inch towards the open grave. With an almighty heave, I roll the body off, and into the hole. As it hits the bottom, one of the bin bags rips completely apart and exposes the top half of the torso. I reel backwards. WTF. WTF.

My legs are giving up the ghost. The Nazi commander is about to shoot me, and shove me in to lie alongside.

I somehow hold myself together, and concentrate on counting out ten pieces of wood from the neatly stacked pile. That should be enough to cover up the makeshift tomb.

First, I have to throw the soil back in to cover up the body, before laying the planks on top. I'll concrete over in the days to come. When I get peace, and an opportunity.

As I shovel back the dirt, I dare to hum.

The job is nearly done.

1

FLO

It takes me a minute or two to work out what I'm looking at. I have to sit down, peel my eyes away from the runway. The plane is already preparing for take-off. OMG.

The pictures on the phone I'm using are grainy. It's a cheap burner phone, but the pictures are getting through. One after another. I hold the phone up, peer at the images from every angle, zooming in and out. As I try to digest what I'm looking at, several videos follow. They're even worse. I watch them several times, before I manage to stand up again.

My legs are like jelly, and I'm coming over hot and nauseous. I move back to the long expanse of window, and shield my eyes against the glare of the sun. Ciara is sitting at the front of the plane. She waved out of the small porthole near the cockpit only five minutes ago, before the plane began to taxi.

I like a window seat. I remember her talking out loud as she filled in the online booking form. She was quick at entering in her card details, and before I knew it, she'd clicked *Buy Now*.

'First on, first off. That's why I sit at the front. And being near the toilet has its advantages.' She giggled, and shut down her laptop.

As her left hand waved through the porthole, her right hand must have been busy on the phone. Images are still pinging onto my burner. Each new shot taken from a different angle. They look like edited stills of the accompanying videos.

But she's now airborne, heading across the Irish Sea to England. To stay at my home. With my husband.

I stare out the window. The shock at what I've seen is turning my insides to liquid. I make a dash for the ladies' in the corner of the airport lounge, and get there just in time.

I reach a cubicle, somehow secure the bolt, before I throw up. When I collapse on the toilet seat, my body is shaking so badly I can hardly hold the phone. Ten minutes pass before I manage to reload the images.

The short reels of video footage were recorded five minutes apart. This time I notice the red seconds counting down in the top left-hand corner of the recordings. Not only have I evidence of a crime, but I have concise confirmation of the time and date, and how long it took to carry it out.

My husband, Ryan, is clearly visible as the perpetrator. He looks so unemotional, that he's hard to recognise. But after ten years of marriage, I know it's him. Although the knowledge doesn't stop me squinting, praying I've got it wrong.

In the first recording, he's carrying out the crime, calmly over-powering his hysterical weakened victim. In the second, he sets about tidying up the scene. He checks all round to see if he's left any clues. I can almost feel the relief in his features when he's finished. Is he smiling? He can't be, surely not. In the last video he unlocks the door, and with a quick backward glance, closes it firmly after him. Yes, he's got a definite curl on his lips, and it's not my imagination. Holy shit.

How did Ciara get these videos? They were taken years ago? Why now? She hasn't sent any messages attached to the pictures and videos, so what does she want?

I stagger outside towards the taxi rank. I can hardly breathe, and am so light-headed I'm scared I'll collapse.

What the hell do you do when you discover that your husband is a cold-blooded murderer? And you had absolutely no idea.

2

FLO

By the time the taxi drops me off at the guest house, I'm seriously freaking out.

I need food, but am far too nauseous to eat, and head for the beach at Ballyholme instead. I need to gulp down fresh air, to help me think. I'm dizzy through shock.

As I climb down onto the sand, I check the time. The plane should have landed at Luton half an hour ago. I take out the cheap phone. Why the hell did I hand over my Apple iPhone so willingly to Ciara? It was all part of *the ruse*, as she called it. I also handed over keys to both the house, and my red Audi.

I'm so fuzzy brained, it's hard to remember exactly what *the ruse* was. One thing I do remember is that Ciara agreed, once she had my iPhone, that she'd take my calls. Day or night. Twenty-four-seven.

'I'll pop outside, I promise. Whenever you call, I'll sneak out the back if Ryan's around. Don't worry I'll keep you posted. It'll be fun. Let's enjoy ourselves.' Her voice purrs in my head. Cat and cream.

I stab viciously at the screen, and try the number over and

over. At least six times. My first two attempts get cut off after three rings, and now it's going straight to voicemail. Why won't she pick up? I leave a couple of garbled messages. I want to scream down the phone, as it's an effort to stay calm. I need to know what's going on.

I'm dripping in perspiration, although the wind from the sea is biting. It cuts through to my bones, and the salt–sand cocktail is seriously irritating my nose. I blast out a ferocious sneeze, which sends a group of squawking seagulls catapulting.

Ciara will soon be at our house. Ryan's and my house. Another hour, two hours tops. Surely she'll pick up before Ryan gets back from work.

I pick my way through the water rivulets criss-crossing the sodden sand. The questions are going round in circles. The pictures Ciara has sent have thrown up a whole can of worms. I thought I knew Ryan. Even after he cheated, I thought he was a pretty open book. Could I have been that wrong?

I've spent the last three months, since I walked out, wondering if I'll ever be able to forgive him for cheating. He strayed only the once, after all, when he had a bunk up with Olivia, our neighbour. In her back garden of all places.

How can I be certain there weren't other times? Does the number of times really matter though? Is a one-night stand any worse than a full-blown affair? Is a single murder pitted against multiple crimes of a serial killer any less grave? That's why I haven't rushed back. I can't decide if I can forgive him. I'm like a one-woman hung jury.

Ryan would often stay late at work. I remember our first Christmas together as a married couple. It was early December, and Ryan announced his company's festive bash for clients and employees was coming up.

'What about wives? Husbands? Aren't we invited?' I was

chomping at the bit to have some fun, and I hadn't met his colleagues.

'You can come. But they're all pretty boring, to be honest. I'll not stay late.'

Put like that, I took the hint. Thinking about it now, did he check his appearance once too often before he left? And 2 a.m. wasn't coming straight home.

I want to trust Ryan. Our marriage was built on compromise, and trust. I was so happy in the early days, and so totally in love. He was amazing when it came to my OCD. He was really calm when I wouldn't let things rest. He seemed to understand, and I loved him even more. If that was possible.

I used to go back inside the house, several times, before we could drive away. Even on a trip to the supermarket, I'd have to double-check all the taps were turned off, all the appliances unplugged. The furthest Ryan ever got to telling me off, was to suggest a therapist.

As I squelch across a rancid sea drain, pinching my nostrils against the stench of rotting seaweed, I start to wonder if Ryan really does go into the office to catch up on work the first Saturday of every month. The thought agitates me even more, as I pick up flattened stones and skim them across the shallows.

I no longer know what to think. The videos of him committing murder is a whole new ball game. His one-night stand now seems almost trivial. Like he'd shoplifted sweets from the corner shop.

3

FLO

I clamber across the concrete groynes sunk into the beach at regular intervals. They're like dead people face downwards in the sand. I shield my eyes and look out across the ocean. Ryan told me Scotland is visible on a clear day. No chance today as the weather is in default mode, grey and damp.

I battle on towards the rocky outcrop which marks the end of the desolate stretch of sandy beach. The rocks are covered in gorse, a yellow blanket of spiky thorns.

'We could borrow some binoculars and do a spot of birdwatching,' Ryan had suggested. He was so desperate for me to love the place. Ballyholme was where he was born.

The heavy sky, laden with moisture, makes me wish I'd escaped to the bikini clad tropics and lain topless on a scorching beach. A thick novel in one hand and a glass of chilled Pinot in the other.

I chose the desolation of County Down deliberately. Bleakness is good company for a broken heart. I wasn't ready to forgive and forget. I wanted to work things out.

The beach today certainly lacks bustle, that's for sure. The only sign of life is a lone dog walker; a speck in the distance. I pick my way across the seaweed booby traps, and think of the book, *The Road*, where father and son walk the earth searching for signs of life after a catastrophe has laid waste to the planet.

Inching forward, I keep checking the cheap mobile with its dearth of sparkly stars. It's matt black with tinny reception and poor resolution. It's so small it's hard to keep hold of.

'A burner phone. That's what you'll need,' Ciara confided, as if we were embarking on some seedy covert mission. Maybe it was pretty seedy, but it was all meant as a joke. Payback against my husband, albeit payback with a difference.

Ciara's cackling laugh sucked me into the *fun idea*.

'I'll be such a laugh. All girls together.' She hugged me. Who was I to question her enthusiasm, even when the doubts came creeping in.

But now I'm doubting everything. Did she have an agenda all along, other than playing the part of new best friend, and trying to cheer me up? Who the heck is she, and where did she get the photos?

It could be the biting wind, or the salty air, but I feel tears dribble down my cheeks. I use frozen fingers to wipe them away, but can't stop the flow. It's lucky there's no one around because I suddenly start to sob. Large, uncontrolled convulsions.

I'm absolutely on my own. No idea what to do.

4

FLO

My mind goes back to the first time I met Ciara.

I was having a glass of wine in The Sailors Arms when Ciara waltzed in. She seemed good friends with Patrick, and I spent a few weeks trying to forget how her lips lingered on his cheek. She was so at ease with him, uncomfortably familiar.

Patrick has the patience of a saint, tells me he's going nowhere. He's been more than a distraction since I arrived in Northern Ireland. He's handsome, fun, and single. Problem is, I'm still married, and reluctant to jump too quickly into a new relationship. But he's hard to resist with his wicked twinkle, and charisma.

'Saint Patrick. That's me,' he jests. But he's struggling. It's his puppy dog eyes.

I can't sleep with him, not until I've seen Ryan again, even if it is to end it all. But Patrick is so hot, that it's really tough.

'Hi. Mind if I join you?' Ciara asked that first night she appeared.

I was sitting by the open fire, playing Wordle. Waffle Wordle. Antiwordle. Octordle. Ryan puts the addictive game playing down to my OCD. I play so many bloody games, one after another. At least I deleted Candy Crush when I saw sweets in my sleep.

'It helps me relax,' I told him, but Ryan didn't get it, and never joined in. My husband doesn't like competition, especially if there's the slightest chance of defeat.

'Yes. The seat's free,' I said to Ciara, reluctantly tearing my eyes from the screen.

'Wordle?' she asked, looking over my shoulder. Her closeness made me stiffen. I nodded, not keen on random conversation.

'I'm Ciara,' she said, stretching her long legs out in front of the flames. Even when the logs spat, she held her ground. She was so relaxed, even back then.

I remember wanting to get up, tell Patrick I'd see him later, when he suddenly appeared and asked Ciara and I what we'd like to drink.

'My treat, ladies,' he said. His eyes twinkled. He knew Ciara well, that much was obvious. I put it down to being a small pub, in a small town, and The Sailors Arms being her local.

I winced when Patrick laid a hand on her shoulder, and asked if she'd like her usual. Then he looked from one of us to the other, and back again.

I'd forgotten all this until now. It suddenly seems important, yet I've no idea why.

'You two look so alike. Check in the mirror,' he said, pointing at the glass over the hearth.

'Jeez, Patrick. Give us a break,' Ciara said. She looked away from Patrick, and turned her attention my way.

'What's your name again?' She wasn't going anywhere.

'Flo. Flo Bartlam.'

'Go on, you two. Have a look in the mirror,' Patrick repeated. 'Don't you see it?'

We stood up, Ciara placed a friendly arm around my shoulder, and we stared into the glass. I did see the resemblance, but nothing out of the ordinary. We both have long hair, shoulder length. Straight. She's a couple of inches taller, and her skin is paler. Almost translucent. Strange, I'm the one with the freckles.

'The Irish are usually the ones with freckles,' she said. 'Are you from Ireland originally? Scotland?'

The questions seemed rather random. But they're coming back. She asked if I'd been to Bangor before. She then asked why I was in Ballyholme.

'Bloody godforsaken hole. A strange place to come for a holiday. How have you ended up here?'

The first time I met Ciara, I wasn't in the mood to share. Things were still raw, and the familiarity between her and Patrick didn't rest easy.

'It's a long story,' I said. 'Another time.'

'I'll keep you to that,' she said.

And she did. Ciara is good at getting what she wants. Before I knew it, I was seeing more of her than I was of Patrick. She was so at ease, familiar. Like a long-lost friend. And in no time at all, she knew my life history. If felt good to talk.

It hits me that maybe she already knew who I was.

5

CIARA

I skid into the pits. Flo's Audi is a mean machine. The sort of car I've always wanted. I test the brakes, let the car swivel on the gravel. I park it at an angle, with the windows cracked. Left side half an inch, right side a couple of inches. Let's get the party started.

The car is the first thing Ryan will see when he gets home. He's in for a shock is all I can say. Flo suffers from OCD, and never parks her car at an angle. She's a talker, and shared lots of secrets. She pops out around bedtime to make sure she's remembered to lock the car. How weird is that?

Another thing she has a phobia about is opened windows. She keeps all the windows in her house closed. Even in the summer. When I get inside, it'll be the first thing I'll do, fling them wide.

'I'm scared of burglars, animals getting in. Ryan thinks I'm mad,' Flo confided.

'Typical men. They're far too trusting.' I agreed with her of course. What else was I going to do? Flo is certainly too trusting, that's for sure. Mother would use the word 'green' for girls who were gullible.

Before I get out of the car, I take in what is to be my new

home. *Tall Trees.* The trees must be round the back of the house because the front is void of trees, and there's a clinical lack of greenery.

The square-fronted house is really symmetrical. It was Flo's choice, apparently. It looks like a child's drawing of a happy family home. Four windows, a door bang centre, with a spiky sun top right and tufted green lawn bottom left. Two circular Georgian pillars, one either side of the door, lend it a faux grandeur. Okay, the sun's hiding for now, but it's all pretty perfect, albeit in an artificial way.

'Wait till you get round the back, though. It's so secluded, that I can even sunbathe topless.' Flo whooped when she shared all, her eyes glazing over in the telling.

'I don't need to pack a bikini then,' I said, trying to nudge away her tears.

'Ryan and I planned to put decking round the back. A place to entertain friends in summer.' The tears rolled down her cheeks.

'Maybe you'll still put it in. Give it time.' I flung my arms round her, gave her a huge bear hug, which seemed to stem the flow.

I dig out the front door key, and lift out my suitcase from the boot. It weighs a ton. Flo did comment that I'd packed a lot for only a few days. I almost forget to take out the shopping bags. They're in the passenger footwell. I made a long *to-buy* list on the plane, and think I've got it all. Even the meat which was pre-ordered three days ago.

I look round the street, but it's deserted. No sign of the nosy neighbours. I made another list of who lives where. Their names, ages, number of children. I even know which house is Olivia's. She's the woman Ryan slept with. Flo told me so much about the neighbours, I feel I know them personally.

'Living at the top of Hillside Gardens is great. We can look down at what's going on, but it's nice and quiet at the top.' When

Flo shared, I thought of kings and castles. But she's right. The house is perched above the others, and has a great vibe about it.

I head for the front door, and once inside, I key in the alarm code. It's eerily quiet, and the house has that unlived-in feel as if it's up for sale. There's no sign of mess.

I dump my bag in the hall, and take myself on a guided tour of downstairs. The lounge, the cloakroom, and the kitchen. Wow. The kitchen is huge. The rest of the downstairs could fit inside the extended space.

'We live in the kitchen. We eat, drink, talk, entertain in the kitchen. It's open plan, and it's where the action is,' Flo announced. She and Ryan had knocked down walls, and extended outwards when they moved in.

'We built our own Aladdin's cave,' she said. She was a bit smug, but I can see why. It's amazing. I get why they live in the kitchen.

A large outside patio is accessed through huge glass doors that extend all the way along the back side of the house. There's so much space, you could entertain the whole street.

It's nearly midday. Ryan usually gets back around six, but he'll likely get back early, because Flo texted a couple of days ago to say she was coming home. She used her iPhone, before she handed it over to me.

Once I've unpacked, I need to prepare supper. Cut up the rabbit, chop the vegetables, and get the stew bubbling.

If I'm to be Ryan's stand-in wife, I need to get a move on.

6

CIARA

It's exactly 5.20, and I can see Ryan through the kitchen window from where I'm standing off to one side.

He's gawping at the open window. He'll be wondering why it's open, and how Flo managed to get it open. It was bloody tough, but I had to let the steam out, otherwise the smoke alarm would have gone off.

Apparently, a few months back the window frames had been repainted and thrown wide to expel the toxins. The Barratts' cat had crawled along the ledge, sneaked in, and lashed its tongue across cold chicken. Flo had slammed the windows shut, and in so doing, the wet paint stuck like superglue.

'Ha. Ryan won't be able to open them any more,' she laughed.

Flo doesn't do animals. It's part of her OCD. Well, that's her excuse. Something to do with the hairs, and fear of deadly diseases carried in their faeces. Ryan would love a big dog to lollop through the park with on a crisp, bright winter's morning. I'm with him on that, as I love dogs.

I found a very sharp-bladed Stanley knife in a drawer by the sink, and used it to slit the seal, cutting a finger in the process. I had a good root around the house, upstairs and down, and found plasters in the main bathroom cupboard. There's everything in there. The contents of the medicine chest are meticulously labelled, and alphabetically arranged. In fact, every room is spotlessly kept, not a thing out of place.

Ryan hasn't moved. He's standing so still, I imagine I hear him breathe. He's clutching a laptop case in one hand, and a bunch of red roses in the other.

I freeze when he takes a small step forward, but he stops again. Jeez. Get a move on. He seems to be sniffing something. A familiar smell. It could be the honeysuckle climbing up the trellis by the front door. I smelled it when I arrived. Or perhaps he can smell Flo's perfume, Midnight Burn, that I sprayed all over my body earlier. It's so strong, it's likely wafting through the window.

I slide away from the window, and with my back to the kitchen door, I take up position by the Aga. If Ryan looks through the window before he comes into the house, he'll see me at work. He'll be so convinced that I'm his wife that he'll be doubly shocked when I eventually face him.

I'm wearing a blinding white T-shirt to showcase my suntan. Ryan will wonder why his wife is so brown. Flo uses Factor 50, and she keeps her freckles religiously covered up.

I've coated my arms with body oil, which I found in the bathroom under M for moisturisers. I'm really glad I work out, as I'm toned, and ready for action. Patrick jokes that I should apply for *Love Island*.

Ryan has reached the front door, which, like the window, is also ajar. He'll be wondering why the heck Flo hasn't closed it. He's now in the hall. I wonder if he'll notice the gap above the hall table where there was a picture of him and Flo skiing, in flash gear and goggles. It's now under the stairs.

My heart is thumping. I'm that nervous, and excited. What the heck will he do, when he realises it's not his wife cooking him his favourite rabbit stew?

I could be the bunny boiler.

7

CIARA

It's tempting to call out. Welcome him home, make him get a move on, but I don't want to warn him that I might not be who he's expecting. He must be really nervous because he still hasn't appeared. What the heck is he doing?

Flo shared he wasn't as cocky, or as confident as he let on. She told me about when he went parachuting, she watched from 12,500 feet below, and he wouldn't jump. She kept screaming at him to let go. He never did, but together they told all their friends that he had been scared, but had finally found the nerve to plummet to certain death, and it had been the most exhilarating experience of his life. Flo must have really loved him, lying for him like that. I'm not sure I would have.

Then I hear him shuffle around in the hall. He plonks something down by the stairs, probably the laptop case he was holding. I wonder if he's still gripping the red roses.

A couple more seconds pass. No doubt he's checking himself in the hall mirror, and suddenly I hear a faint creak from the kitchen door.

I don't turn, but carry on stirring the casserole. I use a small spoon, dip it in to taste for flavour. It's all an act because my mouth tastes of metal.

I wonder how long it will take Ryan to twig. I'm tempted to swivel round and yell 'Gotcha!' I wonder if he's noticed the tattoo on my left shoulder. That's a real telltale sign that I'm not his wife.

'Over my dead body,' Flo told me. She'd never get a tattoo, no matter how tasteful. I think she was overly against them because Olivia had once had a black snake etched above her coccyx. Flo had enthused with her neighbour at the time – 'Wow, that's amazing' – but then shared her derision later on with Ryan.

I'm glad I've laid the table as if for a special occasion. Scented candles, fancy wine flutes I found in the back of a cupboard, and white and gold serviettes. If Ryan's unsure of why Flo has come back, the sight will be like music to his ears.

I can almost hear his heartbeat ratchet up. He'll still be expecting to see Flo, because that's what he's been anticipating for the past two days since he got the text saying she was coming home. He'll not be thinking, or seeing straight. It's fun, but I'm grinding my teeth.

I start to count. One, two, three... then I turn round.

'Ryan. Welcome home.'

Why isn't he moving? He looks as if he's having some sort of seizure. Christ, I hope he's not having a heart attack. He's blinking rapidly, and has put a hand over his chest. He falls back against one of the dining chairs, and seems to lose his balance.

'What the fuck. Who the hell are you?' He spits the words, and his face has come over crimson. He looks really angry.

He's going to need to calm down. Instead of stepping forward, I take a couple of steps back.

For a second, I'm really scared.

8

CIARA

He grabs a chair, and points the legs in my direction. I'm not sure why he's shielding himself from me. What does he think I'm going to do? Attack him with a kitchen knife?

'Are you offering me a seat?' I smile, but my voice is definitely wobbly. I need to relax, and get into the part I've been planning for weeks now.

I turn back to the hobs, lift up the wooden spoon and stir. I offer the end for Ryan to taste.

'Here, try. It's really good.'

'Listen. Whoever the hell you are, can you get out of my kitchen. Now.' He plonks the chair down, and has a good look round, before he asks, 'Where's Flo? Is this some sort of game? Where the hell is she?'

He's right. It is some sort of a game, but he'll not find out what sort for quite a while. There's a long way to go.

Flo told me Ryan does so not like surprises. He makes her swear not to take him unawares. It's a major hate of his. Personally, I think it's about not being in control, a definite male trait.

Apparently, on his fortieth birthday, Flo promised no big

surprises. No sneaking in of friends or colleagues waiting for him when he got back from work. She *crossed her heart and hoped to die.* But Flo is sneaky, I've learned that much. Sneaky in a nice way, she said when challenged.

On the night of his birthday, she had a taxi pick them up and drive them to a fancy country hotel outside Cambridge. A romantic weekend for two, she told him. She showed him a new silky nightie she'd bought specially for the occasion.

She kept the ruse going, and enjoyed telling me how she'd really called his bluff. He'd gripped her hand tightly in the cab, kissed her over and over.

By the time they'd reached the hotel, Ryan was relaxed, pleased to be getting out of London. Even when Flo hurried off in front of him, he still had no idea. That's what she told me. As I look at his face now, aghast, unbelieving, I get how she fooled him.

A throng of revellers had popped out when Ryan and Flo entered the bar.

'Happy birthday,' she'd yelled. 'You didn't really think I'd not make a fuss.'

Flo's a schemer. That's for sure, and it looks as if Ryan suspects she's in on whatever is going on now. He's part of the way there. Flo is involved, but not nearly as much as she thinks.

It'll take Flo a long time to work it all out. And Ryan even longer. By then, it'll be too late for both of them.

9

CIARA

I've made a lot of effort in looking good. Time to put it to good use.

'I'm looking good, aren't I?' I ignore Ryan's distress, and pout my lips for a kiss. When he ignores me, I pick up the matches to relight one of the candles. Caked wax has dripped onto the table-cloth, so I use a freshly painted fingernail to scrape at it.

Ryan is staring. When he does speak again, his voice has risen several decibels. A spasm contorts his face as a tic throbs in his right cheek. He's jiggling his fingers up and down, one after the other. It's as if he's checking the blood is still circulating.

'Who the hell are you? What the fuck is going on?'

'Listen, why don't you have a glass of wine, calm down,' I suggest, handing over a filled glass. 'Or do you want to get changed first?'

He usually goes straight upstairs, yells a quick 'Hello. Won't be long,' and reappears some fifteen minutes later. Tonight, there's no routine. He looks exhausted, and it's hard not to feel for him. But I've too much work to do before I'll let him relax.

Suddenly, a phone rings. The ringtone throws me for a second.

'Air on the G String' by Bach. It's Flo's phone, of course, but I still do a double take when it sounds.

Ryan springs to action. He recognises it. The pink sparkly handset vibrates on the edge of the table, and his hand automatically makes a grab for it. I'm too quick, and beat him to it. Before he can react, I accept the call.

'Hang on,' I mouth at Ryan, as I move off towards the patio doors. 'Won't be a moment,' I whisper, covering the mouthpiece.

'Hi, Olivia. It's great to hear, and yes, I'm home. Ryan and I are just about to eat.' I deliberately muffle the words. Olivia is a bit of a cow, so I told Flo I'd play her as well. Olivia won't suspect she's not speaking to Flo if I talk quietly enough.

'Maybe tomorrow,' I tell her. I haven't quite decided how to play Olivia, but I'll pop across the road and meet her when I'm ready. I try to sound conspiratorial. As if we're sharing a secret. It's for Ryan's benefit, of course, as he'll freak even more if he thinks I know Olivia.

I can feel Ryan staring at me. His tension is boring into my back. I let Olivia talk, and she certainly rambles. I suspect she's trying to win Flo round by her gushing welcome home. She's sorry for what she did, or at least desperate for Flo to think she's sorry, and to forgive her.

'No problem. Speak later. Yes, it's good to be home.' With that I swipe the phone off, and dare to turn round.

Ryan edges uncomfortably close. His eyes are screwed into slits, as if he's trying to focus on some part of my face. Looking for some sort of clue.

Flo has a miniscule scar jeering over her left eye. Ryan is peering at my left eye, as if he's looking for it. It's rather scary letting him stare. I know my skin is very different in texture to Flo's. Hers is rich with freckles, but mine is Irish white, almost opaque

I've been told. I don't tan my face, just keep my body a golden colour.

He now looks all around the kitchen, as if he's waiting for Flo to suddenly jump out.

'Listen. Whoever you are, and whatever the game, I'm going to call the police. I'm going upstairs to change, and when I come down you'd better tell me exactly what's going on. Or else. Get it?' He spits out the words. If he hurled a glass or two across the room, I wouldn't be surprised. He's beyond angry. His jaw is clenched, and sweat is pooling on his hairline.

'Okay. Don't be long.' I try to keep my voice calm, but it's bloody hard.

This guy has serious anger issues, that's for sure.

10

FLO

I'm now soaking, frozen to the core, as I trudge further away from Bangor. If I felt desolate when Ryan slept with Olivia, this is on a whole new scale.

Not long after meeting Ciara, we came up with a *#MeToo* endeavour plan. Well, she came up with it, and told me it would be fun. Why didn't I question it more?

'All girls together,' she said. 'Pay him back, and enjoy ourselves. What do you say?'

It sounded pretty innocent. Ciara squealed, clapped her hands together, as the plan took shape.

The idea was simple. To rattle my husband's cage, payback with a difference. It would give me time to decide what the future held, as I still wasn't sure whether to give him a second chance. Although since meeting Patrick, I've been more tempted to move on.

At the beginning, Ciara made it all seem like a harmless bit of fun. Misgivings only began to rumble as the days passed. I didn't want to piss Ciara off, or seem churlish, by backing off. She took on the role of organiser as well as BFF (best friend forever). When she declared that I was her new BFF, who was I to knock her back?

It felt good to be liked. Ciara was non-judgemental, didn't know too much about my background, and there was no doubt I was in need of a confidence boost. Ciara is very persuasive. She's got a raucous laugh, and is self-deprecating to a fault. She certainly laughs at herself.

'If you can't take it, don't dish it out,' she said. I liked her honesty. Why the hell didn't I question it? Was she playing me the whole time?

Ciara read me well, no doubt about it. I was desperate for support, and for confirmation that I wasn't to blame for Ryan's infidelity. I have no proof that Ryan strayed more than once, but Ciara made me believe it didn't really matter.

'Surely, once is bad enough,' she said. When I dithered, she was quick to come up with the plan. 'Let's enjoy ourselves in the meantime.' And that was it. I gave in.

In return for helping me get payback, she was thrilled when I said she could stay at our house, and take in the sights of London. Free board and lodgings. She'd wind Ryan up, and keep me posted.

The point at which I should have pulled the plug was when she giggled, and wondered aloud if he might dare make a pass at her.

'If he does, we've got our answer,' she said, clapping her hands together.

Oh my God. Was I really that naive?

A sudden shrill pulse pierces the air. It's my phone. It'll be her. Yes. Yes. Yes.

I scrabble around in my pocket to dig out the phone. It's hard to hold, my fingers are so damp. They've turned blue, and the fingertips white. I flick and flick at sand grains speckled across the screen.

It'll be Ciara. I'm so relieved that I let out an enormous puff of air. I shouldn't have worried. It'll have been too difficult for her to speak before. Relief washes over me, and I visualise Ciara's smiling face. All will be forgiven in a heartbeat. Perhaps, I might even forgive Ryan. Who knows?

When I finally clear the screen, it shows up *Number Unknown*. My own number would show up if the call were from my iPhone. Ciara suggested if she borrowed my iPhone, used it in front of Ryan, it would add depth to the ruse.

'He'll wonder where you are. Why I've got your phone. He'll really freak if I don't tell him why. Maybe he'll think you've been kidnapped, had your phone stolen. Come on. You know it makes sense.' I can hear her now.

Then it hits me. It'll be Ryan calling. Perhaps he got this number by checking recent calls on my iPhone when Ciara wasn't looking. But why isn't his number showing up? Maybe he's using another phone, a new burner so we can play the game of covert calls together. My mind is all over the place.

Funny how many thoughts you can have in such a short space. It's to do with heightened senses. Maybe Ryan just wants to ask me to come home, and at this moment, I'd probably agree.

I finally press accept and wait for the caller to speak first.

'Flo? Are you there? Can you hear me?' My stomach plummets with disappointment when I hear it's Patrick. I'm usually so pleased to hear from him.

'Hi. The line's really bad,' I say. I hold the phone out towards the ocean, let in the swishing sounds. 'What's happened to your phone?' I ask, my voice flat.

'Someone nicked it last night. I left it on the bar, next thing it was gone. This is a spare. Where are you?'

Patrick is persistent. He's really keen, and I so don't want to hurt him. I was slowly letting him in, before Ciara came along.

'Sorry, I can't hear you properly.'

A squeal of mewing seagulls fills the air, and I swipe the screen blank. I can't talk to Patrick. Not now.

I need time to think, and I don't want to block up my number in case Ciara tries to get through.

Patrick calls twice more, and that's when I start to cry again. What the hell am I going to do?

11

FLO

I perch on the flat edge of a slimy boulder near the water's edge, and let the water lap round my feet. My trainers are soaked through.

I could phone Ryan, but what would I say? I need to be cautious, until I know what's going on. What Ciara is planning.

It's not easy sending emails on the burner. The screen is so small, but I persevere. I'm suddenly overcome with a weird sense of loyalty to Ryan. Goodness knows how far Ciara has gone with the charade, but Ryan will be freaking out. He hates surprises.

Ciara and I planned that I would send him a cryptic email. Something that would make Ryan think I was in trouble. We giggled at the wording. At the time, Ciara must have known what Ryan had done, that he was a murderer. But I didn't.

The email wording, as per her concoction, is clever, I'll give her that. It's cryptic enough to stop Ryan going to the police.

I stick to the planned text, as I'm scared of what Ciara might do if I change tack. She could be planning anything.

RE: COMING HOME

gowiththeflo32@hotmail.com
Sent: Friday 2 July 15.00
To: Ryan Bartlam
Ryan
Sorry. I'm not coming back. It's complicated. Whatever you do, don't go to the police.
Let her stay. You need to trust me on this.
Flo

I bite down on my thumbnail, and my feet jitter in the water. My jeans are now also drenched, and I feel as if I'm submerged in a cold bath. My once pristine trainers are a murky shade of grey. At least they match the weather.

Ryan's mother described Bangor as a 'dank, dull, dripping, godforsaken hole'. She never stopped moaning in her high-pitched whiny voice. Bitter Lemon, I called her. Ryan chuckled, but wouldn't call her that. He certainly had a misplaced sense of loyalty, and I could have come up with a hundred far worse names.

I check my Fitbit. I've only done 8,200 steps. I need to get up to 10,000 before five o'clock. Another 1,800 to go.

'Does it matter when you do the steps?' Ryan would ask.

'Yes. If I do 10,000 steps before five, I'll be halfway there.'

I'd pound up and down the stairs after supper, until I reached my daily goal. Ryan would let me get on with it, turning up the telly to block out the noise. He was so patient.

For ten minutes I stare at the screen. Ryan is a phone hugger, and I can't imagine him without his phone, unless he left it at work in his hurry to get home, but I know I'm grasping at straws. I'm certain he'll hurry home, since he got the text a couple of days ago telling him I was on my way. Although he might stop by the pub and have a couple for Dutch courage.

My mind is all over the place. What the hell have I done? I

should have gone home. Talked things through, and we might have worked things out.

I slither off the boulder, wobble, and nearly topple into the ocean.

Maybe it wouldn't be such a bad thing.

12

FLO

As I head back to the guest house, I'm forced off the beach. The tide is now lapping against the green slimy sea wall, and I clamber up the steep set of steps that lead to the Esplanade.

I think of the blurb I googled the first time I came to Bally-holme. To meet Ryan's mother.

Handsome terraced houses along the Esplanade provide a pleasant backdrop to a bracing walk towards Ballymacormick Point.
Paddle in the surf and build sandcastles on the beach.
Join the windsurfers and skim along the waves in the breeze. Perfect for a family day out with bucket and spade.

Ryan said I'd love it here. As I push forward against the wind, more gale force than sea breeze, I remember how utopian I'd found it. That was until I met his mother. She lurked in a dark corner of paradise.

There's not a soul around. Grand buildings line my route, but no one's knocking on neighbours' doors to borrow milk or sugar lumps. It's like an exclusive ghost town.

'Everyone is in the pub,' Ryan joked, the first time we walked this route. Back then, it sounded like a joke. Now I'm not so sure, as I'm certainly in need of a drink.

I pull my hoodie tighter, and speed up. I need to get back.

By the front entrance to the guest house, I check my Fitbit: 9,880 steps. I walk right, left, and back again until I reach 10k. Then I step inside.

* * *

The first thing I do, is take a scalding shower. I stand until my body comes back to life.

I towel, blow-dry my hair with a seriously dangerous hairdryer attached to a faulty plug, then flop onto the bed. I prop my head against the hard heap of pillows. Hypo-allergenic.

My request for non-feather bedding sent Damian, the hall porter, into Bangor for replacements. I smack the pillows to plump them up, but they're like concrete, and aren't helping a building migraine. The thunder of waves crashing against the sea wall outside isn't helping either.

I hug my arms round my body, and imagine an undersea earthquake might have triggered a tsunami, and that the coastline of County Down will soon be obliterated.

I slide off the bed, and go to try and close the sash window. It's stuck, an inch from the bottom. Outside is dark and menacing, as the storm approaches. The sun has been obliterated by an ebony roof which covers the length of Ballyholme Beach.

There's still no word from Ryan. No response to the email, and I keep checking. As the minutes tick by, part of me is desperate to phone him. Speak to him. The more angry I get with Ciara, the more I want to side with Ryan. Confused doesn't even touch the surface. Perhaps I should forgive him. Yes, perhaps we could try again, maybe move away, and never have to see Olivia again. Away from the constant reminder of his infidelity.

But he's a murderer. WTF. That is something else entirely.

13

FLO

I swallow down a couple of paracetamol, and fall into a fitful sleep.

It's past nine when I check the time again. My head is fuzzy, and I need to get out. Also, I've got to see Patrick. His final message was a row of sad emojis.

I tug a woollen jumper over my head, pick up my raincoat, and opt for my sturdy walking boots. The guest house is as quiet as the seafront, and there's no sign of Damian when I reach the lobby.

I'm greeted by a torrential sheet of rain, as I hover on the front step leading down to the pavement. A sane person would duck back inside. But time isn't on my side.

I turn left, and let the rain smash against my back as I battle along the coast road in the direction of Bangor town centre. It's not far until I reach the corner of Ballyhill Gardens, and The Sailors Arms pub. It's where I met Patrick. And Ciara.

The saloon is tucked into what was once someone's living room. From outside, the only thing that sets it apart from the terraced houses either side, is the full-frontal glass window which runs floor to ceiling. Lack of curtains showcase the jollity inside, and it's certainly busier than on the street.

The I is pretty homely. Dark wooden tables and chairs are crammed into the space, and a worn maroon and yellow carpet with a swirling pattern reminds me of my grandmother's living room.

A solid mahogany bar counter stretches from one side of the room to the other, and looks as if it's supporting the bowed walls. Green, white and gold towelling runners remind me I'm in Ireland. As if I could forget.

Through the window, I watch Patrick scurry back and forth. He's perfected the art of balancing plates of food along both arms, and he's pretty agile when it comes to side-stepping the salivating dogs. Even from where I'm standing, the now familiar smell of Irish stew wafts through to the street.

Funny, but I'm watching Patrick for signs, although I'm not sure what I'm looking for. His face lights up when he spots me, and he mouths, 'Come in,' tilting his head towards the entrance. I instantly feel guilty. Why am I doubting this guy? He's been there for me. I've told him all about Ryan's sordid little fling, and Patrick has been a broad set of shoulders. He's also patient, and says he'll wait for me. He makes me feel special, loved, the way Ryan used to.

I haven't told him about Ciara's and my ruse. We decided our #MeToo ruse was for ladies only.

'No need to tell Patrick,' Ciara said. 'He wouldn't approve. He hates women's causes.' She seemed to know Patrick well, but then she's known him much longer than I have.

Maybe she *did* tell him of our plan. She's a talker, but if she did, would he know about the *change of plan*? Her *change of plan*, whatever it is. Does he know about the videos she threw at me as her plane lifted off?

I have so many questions, that I don't know where to start.

14

FLO

Patrick winks as I stagger, padded like a Sherpa, through the heavy doors. A glass panel in the centre is etched with a harp and lets the punters know they're definitely not in Scotland.

He nods towards the table by the window. In the centre is a 'reserved' sign, along with a single red rose in a cracked vase. Patrick guessed I'd show.

His pale face is flushed, and his thick caterpillar brows dip in the middle. But *the Irish eyes are smiling*. Humour oozes from his brown eyes, and his looks sizzle with danger. He's so damn attractive, I've no idea how I've resisted sleeping with him. He's persistent, as well as patient, and is the most perfect guy I've met. Apart from Ryan, who once seemed so perfect.

'I'll just be a few minutes. Make yourself at home,' Patrick calls over. He's stacking empty glasses, and swears under his breath when slops spill onto the floor.

'Holy shit,' he mumbles, rolling his eyes and grinning at me. 'Usual?' he asks. 'House white?'

I give him a thumbs up, before I take off my coat, hat and gloves, and pull out a chair. There's one either side of the table, but

I always sit in the same one. The one on the right, as right is my *go-to* side.

'What's a *go-to* side? Can't we just sit down?' I rewind Ryan in my head. He would humour me, and soon he knew to pick the *left* of everything. Chairs, ends of sofas, seats on planes, and sides in bed.

Ryan accepts I need to be on the right. He gives in to my quirks, tries to keep me happy, but also knows he doesn't have a choice.

It's weird, especially tonight, sitting in the exact same spot that Ryan and I shared seven years ago. Almost to the day. I rest my elbows on the table, drop my head into my hands, and stare out at the gloom. The lighthouse is flickering, like it did that first time.

'Look at that view,' Ryan had said. 'You'll never see that in London. Cheers. Here's to Ireland.'

We'd chinked glasses. Nothing about the place has really changed, at least in the physical sense, yet everything is different.

Patrick disappears to get the drinks, and to clock off work for the evening. He likes being the boss.

'More freedom to do what you fancy,' he says. But work's his life. He's at home running a pub. Ciara prefers working behind a bar, helping out with no responsibility. Thinking of her sets me off again.

I realise I haven't checked my phone for the last half-hour, since I left the hotel. I dig it out from my drenched coat pocket. I sit bolt upright when I see the new email, and swallow hard before I read. My legs jiggle furiously, and I realise my body is shaking in time.

Flo

What the hell is going on?? A mad woman is in our house pretending to be you.

What am I supposed to do if I can't go to the police?? She can't stay here.

Call me on my mobile. Now. Please.

Are you in danger? I need to know. Is it money she's after??

Please, I'm begging you. If it's a game you're both playing, just let me know.

But I'm starting to freak in case you're in danger. She's got your passport. Did you know?

Get back to me. I'll keep my phone close.

Ryan xx

P.S. I still love you.

'One glass of the house white, madam.'

I swipe the phone off at the sound of Patrick's voice, push my phone to one side.

'Thanks.' My hand shakes when I take the glass.

'You okay? You look a bit peaky,' he asks. Seriously, I feel a lot worse than peaky.

'I'm fine. Just soaked through.'

'Do you want to sit by the fire? Everyone will be gone soon.'

When I shake my head, he sits down opposite. On the chair to the left. He leans across the table, brushes my lips with his, before taking a long swig from his Guinness. His tongue licks off a creamy line of foam which settles on his moustache. He looks tired, but relaxed.

'It's great to see you. I wasn't sure if I'd done something wrong,' he says.

I slump backwards, put my glass down.

'Patrick,' I say. His smile deflates. 'I need to talk to you.'

'Sounds serious. What's up?' He hunches his shoulders, and crosses his arms.

'Ciara. Have you heard from her? Do you know where she is?' I stare at him. He doesn't seem twitchy, more worried that perhaps I might be about to ditch him.

'No. Should I have?'

His eyes are drizzled with concern.

'Did you know she's gone to stay at our house for a few days? Mine and Ryan's house. I haven't had a text or call to say she's arrived.'

'Oh, I didn't know. She said she was off to London to visit a girl-friend, and I know better than to pry. It's not like her not to text though. She's never off her bloody phone.' He puffs exasperated lips.

'I thought I'd have heard from her. Ryan didn't know she was coming, and I didn't tell him. We're still not on speaking terms, as you know. I gave Ciara a key and told her to make herself at home.'

Patrick leans back more easily. He's relieved, nothing more. Ciara didn't share our plan with him, I'm certain. As I watch Patrick for signs, no idea what sort of signs, my stomach lurches. I could really fall for him, but feel a need for caution. I don't know him that well, but I feel I can trust him.

But then I thought I could trust Ciara.

15

FLO

Patrick locks up when the last punter leaves, and pours us both a whiskey nightcap.

The drink helps me unwind, unravel the knots strangling my body. We chat about this and that, and I don't know how I manage to manoeuvre the conversation round to euthanasia. I soon thread in talk of Ryan's mother, who died in an old people's home on the far side of Bangor.

'Ryan's mother struggled towards the end,' I say. I watch Patrick, but he's relaxed, and twiddles with his St Christopher pendant. He doesn't flinch at the direction of the conversation.

'It's tough watching loved ones get old. How did she die?' he asks, twisting the gold chain in his fingers. Round and round.

'She died in Mulberry Lodge nursing home. I think I told you?' I don't say how she died, as I'm curious to hear what he says.

'Old age? Bloody awful places those nursing homes.'

'Natural causes were recorded.' I stare at him. Not a flicker, although he's moved from fiddling with his jewellery to toying with a beer mat, and sliding it from side to side.

'To be honest, I'd put them all out of their misery. I think I'd rather be dead than end up in one of those places.'

The wine suddenly has an acid bite. What's he saying? Does he really mean that? What does he mean?

'Do you agree with euthanasia?'

Ryan talked about it often enough. His mother threatened repeatedly that if he didn't take her home, she'd kill herself. He joked he'd do it for her. Perhaps she ended up begging him for help.

It suddenly hits me, maybe that's what happened. Ryan helped put his mother out of her misery. She hadn't long left to live, as she constantly reminded Ryan. Maybe he finally agreed to end it for her.

'Yes. I'd rather be put out of my misery, than have a slow, painful death,' Patrick says, echoing my thoughts.

A sense of relief that Ryan was likely acting out of mercy should cheer me up. But why aren't I convinced? Assisted suicide is nowhere near as serious as cold-blooded premeditated murder. Oh my God. This could be a whole new ball game. And listening to Patrick's views on euthanasia, I'm even more confused.

Did Ryan commit cold-blooded murder, or did he help his mother die to end her suffering? There's a huge difference, and I need to find out which one it was. The videos of Ryan smothering his mother, the videos Ciara sent, could be telling either story.

* * *

As I put my outer layers back on, Patrick doesn't get up. He's given up asking me to stay the night, or hoping that I might sneak him into the guest house. He knows how to make a really sad face, and regularly stares me down with saucer eyes, but it's still too early days.

'Listen. Why don't we take a trip over to the Copeland Islands tomorrow, or on Sunday? I can get cover for the bar. We could make a day of it,' he suggests.

I smile at him. He deserves so much more than I can give him, but I hesitate only briefly.

'It sounds lovely.'

I don't mention that I mightn't be here in a few days' time. Yet, while I am here, reluctant to fly home, I should try and enjoy myself. Also, I might need Patrick's help.

Although he's looking at me with his sexy eyes, and crooked smile, something is niggling. There's so much I don't know about Patrick, and with everything that's going on, my thoughts are all over the place.

Patrick could be a lifeline, and he could be my future. Why am I worried he might also be my executioner?

16

CIARA

Ryan is so bloody angry. He obviously hasn't got Flo's email yet. Or hasn't read it. Flo must be pretty worried about what I have in mind, or she would surely have tried to ring Ryan, or at least text. They are one of those obsessive texting couples.

She told me that after leaving Ryan, she ghosted him and ignored all his attempts to get in touch. She's a master at text ignoring, apparently. If she was prepared to forgive him, stand by his murder, I'm surprised she hasn't called him. At least she's still in the game because I told her not to. A cryptic email would be enough. That's what we agreed.

I'm not sure what I'd tell the police if Ryan carries through with his threat, and phones them. Leaving now isn't an option, as I've come too far.

Hopefully, once he gets Flo's email, he'll back off. Wait it out, like she tells him. I didn't expect him to be so angry, although I wonder why I didn't as I've witnessed his anger first hand.

A couple of minutes pass, then I creep up the stairs after Ryan. I need to make sure I left the door to the spare bedroom open. My suitcase is on the bed, the pink tortoiseshell one that Flo lent me. Ryan's bound to glance in as he passes.

'He'll recognise the case,' Flo had said.

'How come?'

'When I stormed out, the case burst open before I could hoist it into the boot of my car.'

'Did he help you?'

'No. I told him to piss off, and not to come any closer.'

I patted her on the shoulder, as her bottom lip quivered.

'I don't think I've ever been so mad. I drove like a maniac, the car slithering all over the place,' she said.

I reckon Ryan will recognise the clothes now spilling out of the same case. They're all Flo's. The Nike training gear. The bright orange Lycra top and figure-hugging black pants. Laid out for my evening jog. I'll follow Flo's route, through the rear garden, up to the gate at the end, and along the forest trail. The green route is a five-mile circuit.

Flo runs every evening after supper. Burns the calories, rain or shine. Her obsession for perfection will be a hard act to follow. She never rests until she's done so many steps, always an eye on her Fitbit. It'll take effort, but the more I can be like Ryan's *perfect* wife, the easier it'll be to reach my goal.

I'm definitely a peeping Tom. And good at it. Ryan has no idea I'm watching him through the crack in his half-closed bedroom door. He's tugging at his tie, the knot of which is the size of a walnut, and he can't undo it. I want to help, but not without blowing my cover. He finally manages to push his head through the red noose, before chucking the tie across the room.

He throws open the bedroom window, and sniffs his armpits. I guess the smell's not good, as his body is bathed in sweat. He's standing in nothing but his underpants, and looks drop-dead gorgeous. If I were Flo, I wouldn't have left so quickly. In the looks department, the odds are definitely stacked in his favour. Patrick says I'm bitchy, and hates when I criticise Flo.

Ryan's red and yellow boxer shorts are hilarious. I have to put a hand over my mouth to cap the chuckle. They're woven through with a pattern of classic cars driven by dogs. They were probably a present from Flo, as she said vintage cars are his 'thing'.

Ryan grips the top of the radiator under the window ledge. Even from my position I see his knuckles whiten. He's staring out at the street below. I wonder if he spots Olivia, as I watched her earlier through the kitchen window pottering in her front garden. I bet she still hankers after Ryan.

I suspect he'll swallow his pride soon, and pop across the road to ask Olivia if she knows where Flo is. He'll be curious if his neighbour knows me, as he heard us on the phone. He'll want to find out if she's in on what's going on.

Ryan inhales deeply, and stands very still. That's when I make my move.

'Ryan. Don't worry, I've left my suitcase in the spare room. It's early days.'

'Fuck.' He stubs his toe against the radiator when I speak. 'What the fuck do you mean "early days"? Early days for what? Can you just take your bloody suitcase and get out of my house.'

I think he's mortified at being caught in such ridiculous underpants, because he doesn't know where to look.

'Keep your hair on. Come down and we'll talk. Let's eat first, because I don't know about you, but I'm starving. Aren't you hungry?'

When he glowers at me, I get the hint, and back off.

I pop back into the spare room, and make sure Flo's passport can't be missed. It's on the edge of the bed nearest the door.

17

CIARA

Ryan appears pretty sharply. No sign of the doggy boxers. He's now dressed in a peach linen shirt, and navy chinos. His feet, encased in sliders, are surprisingly white compared to his tanned legs. With so little effort he still manages to pull off a *Love Island* look.

I've already set the vegetables and crisp (the way Ryan likes them) roast potatoes on the table. Homely steam wafts upwards. He checks out the scene with hands stuffed down his shorts.

'Come in. It's all ready,' I say. I keep stirring the large copper casserole with the brass handles. It's Flo's kitchen pride and joy. I can't imagine Flo being able to lift it because it's bloody heavy. I've managed to hoist it off the hob a couple of times, glad that I'm religious about working out with weights.

Flo humours Ryan, and teases him with ruses to strengthen their partnership. She likes to play Jane to his Tarzan. The maiden in distress.

As I hoist the casserole, and get it onto the table, I sense Ryan's eyes on me, as well as on the scene. I've been busy getting to know the kitchen, where things are kept. I've moved smaller plates onto higher shelves, rearranged the glasses, and put my own stamp on how I like things organised.

The table is set for a special occasion. At the back of one cupboard I dug out some slate place mats, along with the white and gold serviettes, which I've folded into a couple of cut-glass wine goblets.

Everything looks perfect. Instead of complimenting my efforts, Ryan comes up to the table, eerily quiet, and yells in my ear.

'Right. You'd better bloody well start talking. Tell me what's going on. Or else...'

He's spitting angry, again. He needs to seriously calm down.

'Okay. Okay. Keep your hair on,' I say. 'Let's sit down. I've gone to a lot of trouble.' My eyes work the table. 'If you're not hungry, I am, and then we can talk.'

I dip a spoon in the casserole, and offer it to Ryan. 'Taste it. What do you think?'

Ryan ignores me, yanks out a chair and flops down at one end of the rectangular table. He could be about to conduct a board meeting.

'What is it?' he asks.

'What's what?' He's determined not to show interest, his voice flat. But at least he's asked.

'What's in the pot?'

Apparently, the first question he asks Flo every night is 'What's cooking?' It drives her mad. But tonight, it's a good question from where I'm standing. At least he may have stopped imagining that I'm some sort of bunny-boiling psychopath. Playing his stand-in wife for a few days is my intention, not slitting his throat with the paring knife.

Before I've a chance to answer, he swivels round in his chair. He must have cricked his neck, because he's wincing, his palm rubbing down one side.

He's heard the music. It's been playing in the background all the time, but it's only just registered. Bruce Springsteen, Leonard Cohen, Bob Dylan, Amy Winehouse. They're Flo's favourite artists. In Bangor, she added Ed Sheeran and George Ezra to her playlist.

Ryan jumps up, and makes a grab for the music speaker.

'Where did you get this?'

Ryan turns the speaker round and round in his fingers, as if looking for clues. He recognises it as Flo's, the one he bought for her.

'It's mine,' I say with a smirk. I shouldn't wind him up any more, but it's so tempting.

And he deserves it. Wait till he hears it's rabbit stew in the pot.

18

CIARA

Ryan makes a grab for me. Not in the way I'd like, but his steel-tipped fingers circle my wrists until he's stemmed the blood flow to my fingers. They turn white pretty quickly.

'Get off me,' I scream, writhing like a snake.

'Not till you tell me what the fuck is going on. I'm tired, and fed up with these bloody charades. If you don't talk, I *am* calling the police. Get it?' He lets go and throws my hands off.

'Loud and clear.' I shake my hands out and rub my wrists.

We take our seats like enemies round a peace-talks' table, no one prepared to give up their tanks.

I serve up in silence, slopping a dollop of stew and vegetables onto the plates.

'To answer your earlier question. It's rabbit stew.' I slide his plate across.

'Whatever,' he says. But he's eyeing the rabbit legs, his favourite bits. He's a dark meat man.

The local butcher, Prime Cuts, has to order rabbit in by special request. It takes three days. Perhaps Ryan is wondering, as he sticks a fork in the meat, how I got it. Another needle to his brain. Let him work it out. Flo let slip the name of the butcher's, so I made sure to call.

'Right. I'm listening.' He pushes his plate to one side, straightens his knife and fork like a truculent schoolboy. *I'm not going to eat my food, unless...*

'Can't you just imagine I'm your wife for now. You might even get used to me. Hmm, this is delicious.' I speak with an overly full mouth. The stew is delicious, if I say so myself, and I'm amazed how well I've followed the recipe, as I'm unadventurous with food. Having Ryan to cook for certainly made me concentrate.

'YOU-ARE-NOT-MY-WIFE.' He enunciates the words as if I'm deaf. 'Is this all Flo's idea? Does she think this is funny?'

'Well, you have been a naughty boy. Haven't you? Not sure I could forgive you.'

'What the fuck has it got to do with you? She's paid you, hasn't she? You're doing this for money.'

His words don't match his expression. He looks bewildered, and gnaws away at the inside of his cheek.

He surely can't think this is Flo's style. To set up a charade for money? I so want to laugh. While he's been yelling, he's lifted up his knife and is jabbing the tip into the slate place mat.

'Why would Flo be after money? If she leaves you, goes for divorce, she'll get half of whatever you've got. And the rest. Certainly easier than playing games.' I sop up the juice with a rounded potato, before spearing a garlic clove, and popping it in my mouth.

'Why then? Why? What's this all about?'

'Hasn't she phoned you?' I doubt he'd be so het up if she had, but I need to know she's not going to double-cross me. Go off at a tangent. We agreed no phone calls. She hasn't phoned Ryan once since she left, so I thought best keep it that way. At least until I get my foot under the table.

I might be sneaky, but then so is Flo. We're not that different. When she found out about Olivia, she didn't let on straight away. Olivia owned up to Flo what had happened between her and Ryan. Probably wanted her side of the story told first, but Flo kept the knowledge close to her chest. It was only when Ryan thought he'd got away with it that she went for the jugular. She got more furious when he tried to blame Olivia.

'She threw herself at me. I was drunk, and you know she's completely mad. It's you I love. It's only ever been you.' This was how Flo told it, using a whiny voice to mimic her husband.

Flo's pretty smug. Thinks she's clever. But who's laughing now?

Ryan shakes his head, still stabbing with the knife. He looks so dejected that I finally throw him the crumb he's after.

'Have you checked your emails? Flo should have been in touch by now.'

'Why hasn't she called me? Doesn't she have a phone?'

'I think she's not that keen on talking. But she promised she'd email if she got the chance.' Might as well let him think Flo is in danger. Or better still, make him angry that his perfect wife is deliberately playing him.

'Is she in danger? Is that it?'

He's already up out of his chair, and racing out of the kitchen.

I hear him trip on the stairs, and suddenly all goes quiet. There's no more creaking, or moving around. As Flo's playlist comes to an end, it's even quieter.

Ryan will be booting up his laptop, and hopefully checking his spam folder.

Part of the plan was to tease Ryan with all sorts of thoughts. If Flo acted weirdly, not true to form, Ryan would get panicky. Any emails from the new, unrecognised Hotmail address would likely go to spam.

'He always checks his emails, clears the spam, before he gets into bed,' Flo confided. I'm not sure whose habits are more rigid, Flo's or Ryan's.

So I helped her set up a new email address: gowiththeflo32@hotmail.com.

She loved it. She shared that she's always telling people to loosen up. Rather hypocritical considering she's wound as tight as a spring. But the unfamiliar address will load on even more questions for Ryan.

I bite on my thumbnail, which is down to the quick, and lick off a small speck of blood. If Flo has followed through, and sent the email, I can begin the next stage of my plan.

It'll be much more fun. I hold my breath, start the count down, and wait for Ryan to reappear.

19

FLO

When all the punters have left the pub, I tell Patrick the sea air has knocked me out, and I need an early night. He admits he's shattered too, and promises to text in the morning.

I button up, say goodnight, and hurry the short distance back to the guest house.If I thought it was cold outside, it's freezing in my room.

A crack in the window frame leaks icy torture through the gap. It's so cold that I've stopped shivering. My body is in rigor mortis.

I brush my teeth, and dive under the duvet, wrapping it tightly round me in the vain hope that I'll fall asleep. But I'm wide awake. I turn from one side to the other, and back again, and am soon checking the time every twenty minutes.

When it gets to 3 a.m., I finally give up. A full moon glowers through the window, and the sight makes me more crazy.

Ryan pooh-poohs the belief that a full moon makes us restless. When I toss and turn in bed, he asks what's up, and scoffs if I mention the moon. But tonight it's sending my thoughts into overdrive.

I get out from under the covers, and plug in the plastic kettle. I rip open a couple of coffee sachets and shake the contents into the mug. Sleep is now impossible, but I don't know what else to do. Despite the anxiety, and the night sweats soaking my nightshirt, the calming effect of the camomile tea bags isn't calling to me.

There have been three more pleading emails from Ryan, following on from the first one I got earlier. The final one demanding more forcefully to know what's going on. He's not in a good place, and I almost feel sorry for him. He'll be crazy not being in control.

My mind skitters back and forth. When I think of him and Olivia, the hurt and fury comes back, and I never want to speak to him again. But Ciara has clouded everything, and I'm struggling with a misplaced sense of loyalty to my husband. It's our marriage after all. Yet Ciara, a complete stranger, has taken control of both our lives.

I reread the last email Ryan has sent.

From: Ryan Bartlam
To: gowiththeflo32@hotmail.com
Flo
Please, please, please get back to me and tell me what's going on.
I had to sit through a bloody supper charade with this woman and still haven't a clue what it's all about. I'm really sorry. If that's what you need to hear, I can't say it enough. If this is about payback, I get it. But if it's not, I'm starting to seriously freak out.
Why can't I go to the police and get rid of her? Are you in danger? I'll give it a couple of days and then I'll have no choice. I'll take my chances if you don't tell me what's going on.
Ryan xx
P.S. How does this woman know I like rabbit? A bit of a long shot that she guessed this was my favourite. It was as tough as old boot btw. Not a patch on yours.

P.P.S. What the hell is her name anyway? I haven't managed to get an
answer out of her.

I told Ciara about the rabbit stew, Ryan's favourite meal. It was
a fun part of the ruse.

'What's wrong with Irish stew?' Ciara had asked.

'You must be joking. Ryan is a real foodie. All things Italian.
Coniglio alla Cacciatora is his absolute favourite. A dish with origins
among the fieldworkers and peasants of northern Italy.' I spelled
the Italian words out for her, but explained that in England we call
it Hunter's rabbit stew.

Dust the rabbit pieces with flour. Heat the oil in a casserole dish and
brown the meat on all sides. Add the garlic and rosemary, fry a little, and
then tip in the wine. Let the alcohol evaporate, before adding the toma-
toes. Cover with the lid, and let it come to the boil, stirring from time to
time. Lower the heat and simmer gently for about an hour.

I'd been drunk when I shared the recipe. It was early days, and
it all seemed so innocent.

Ciara wrote nothing down. I thought her memory must be
good, or she was humouring me with intent to follow through.

Now I'm livid that she's in my house, cooking for my husband,
his favourite dish. What was I thinking?

I close down my laptop, and head for the bathroom. It's only a
coffin-sized cubicle, but the spluttering shower jets soon come to
life. Goosebumps stipple my skin, but the hot water blasts it back
to life.

I towel, pick up my discarded jogging gear, and get up Google
Maps on my phone. There's somewhere I want to go, and I'm much
too edgy to wait for daylight.

It'll take me about twenty minutes to get there. I don't know
what I'll find, but it feels good to be doing something. Anything to
stop the cycle of torture, and indecision.

20

FLO

I sneak out past the night porter, who is asleep behind the reception desk. Faint puffs of air quiver through his rubbery lips, and a sudden guttural blast disturbs the rhythm when I reach the main entrance. But he doesn't wake up.

Outside, I pull my hoodie tight, and decide to stick to the pavement. Despite the full moon reflecting off the water, the narrow sandy beach is unlit, and the tide is in. I can hear the water lapping against the sea wall.

I set off at a light jog, but build speed as I get closer to Bangor. I check my phone, and I've about two miles to go. The address is somewhere near the back of the Boyne Housing Estate.

Each time my foot hits the pavement, it dislodges another thought. They're like flimsy roof tiles. I try and make sense of what's going on. Payback with a difference has turned into a nightmare. Was it all entirely Ciara's idea? Why did I go along with it? I was really angry, but this isn't fun payback. It feels like revenge. I can't remember if I agreed with the plan, or if I was railroaded. Ryan would never believe the latter, that's for sure.

Can't you give an inch? At least now and again. You're so bloody stubborn. I can hear him as I pound the pavement.

Ciara was clever. She fuelled the fire of my confusion. I shared the anger, hurt, doubts. She's a great listener, that's for sure. When she shared that Patrick was smitten, and I should give him a chance, I fell for it. She winked on the word 'smitten'.

'It'll be great to stay in London. Thanks for the invite,' she said. Another hug, and what could I say? 'I'll make Ryan sweat. And don't worry, I'll keep house and he'll not starve.'

I stumble as my foot catches on the edge of a broken slab, and I'm thrown sideways against mesh fencing.

'Shit. Shit. Shit.' The pain shoots through my ankle, up my leg.

I lean heavily against the fence for a few minutes. It feels as if someone has bashed my ankle with a sledgehammer. I dig out my phone, and the lighted screen tells me I've reached my destination.

I peer through the chain-link barrier, gripping tightly, as my ankle is in serious threat of collapse, and I have to bite down against the pain.

The single-storey concrete building looks like a prison. Grey walls, postage-stamp windows, and coiled barbed wire running along the top of the fencing, and I could be outside Wandsworth Prison. I wonder who would want to break in? And no one inside would be able to break out, that's for sure. But the place is deserted.

It's hard to recognise the building, and the garden from the pictures Ryan showed me years ago. My memory of the images is vague, but I remember grass clipped like a croquet lawn. The images helped ease my husband's guilt. He joked that the residents could partake in a gentle game of croquet during the warm, wafting summer breezes. Maybe he never felt guilty. The care home costs were exorbitant, but Ryan didn't bat an eyelid. Only the best for his mother, he told me, but he found it hard to hide the relief that she was to become someone else's problem.

As I stare at the ugly building, the doubts multiply. Ryan locked her up, and hurried back to England with a clear conscience. I can't remember the number of times he flew back to see his mother, but it was enough to ease the guilt, and to check the fees were worth it.

Did he murder his mother to save money? The thought hits like a brick.

Hairs tingle on the back of my neck. Not long after Ryan had moved his mother into Mulberry Lodge Nursing Home, he sent me WhatsApp images he took himself. The realism told a very different story from the glossy brochure. Bent croquet hoops were stacked against a crumbling wall, and the weather was in default mode. Wet, with no hint of summer breezes. Ryan didn't seem particularly worried, just relieved that his mother was being looked after.

The front lawn of what was once Mulberry Lodge Nursing Home is now overrun by straggling weeds and waist-high grasses. To one side of the building, I notice the sign. *For Sale.* Graffitied across the bright orange board, in thick black marker: *LONG LIVE THE IRA.* The past is eerily knocking at the present.

I key in the name and number of the estate agent onto my phone. It looks as if the place has been derelict for some time. Perhaps the residents were moved on to other homes when the place was put up for sale.

Or perhaps they were all murdered.

21

FLO

Daylight is breaking through by the time I turn back. The sun is coming up, and cars begin to rumble along the deserted streets.

My ankle screams in agony as I hobble along. I feel I'm sleep-walking through a nightmare, as macabre images of dead bodies, and fleshless skeletons flicker in and out. A couple of random dog walkers nod as they pass, covered head to toe in thick layers, but the perky day-time greetings are muted. Nods and mumbles are the height of it, as the cold night air has sapped the jollity.

Rogue thoughts squeeze through the pain. I remember Ciara, drunk on excitement from *the plan*, suggesting that perhaps she could seduce Ryan.

'I'll not let him anywhere near me, of course. But if he tries, that'll give you your answer. That he's sooo not to be trusted.'

It didn't seem important. Just another of her wild ideas. 'If he's easily seduced, he's likely strayed more than once.'

No. No. No. She wouldn't try, would she? Perhaps she will seduce Ryan and give me an answer, but not the one she promised. The one that would tell me I had to let him go, that he was a no-good bastard. But another answer. That I needn't bother coming home, because I'd had my chance and my husband has moved on. He's sorry, but he's met someone else.

Inch by inch I shuffle along. My ankle feels as if it's going to burst, and as the pain gets worse, all I can think about is reaching my room. I grip the iron railing on the steps up to the guest house.

It's almost seven o'clock, the lights are on, and Damian is in the lounge tugging at the curtains. He waves, but I keep my head down.

By the time I reach the bedroom, my ankle has swollen like a melon. A wall of suffocating heat hits, as the radiator has come on, and is clunking loudly through effort. I tear off several layers of clothing, and go to the bathroom and dig out a strip of ibuprofen. I swallow a couple of tablets with the dregs of cold coffee, and collapse onto the bed.

I cocoon myself in a swirl of bedding, willing the pain to subside. Not only am I exhausted, but I'm starting to hallucinate. It's a symptom of sleep deprivation, which luckily hasn't yet attacked my memory. I've no trouble remembering everything.

'Give me your passport. That'll really freak Ryan out. He'll think you've been mugged. Or worse. You won't need it to get back to England, and it'll only be for a few days.' Ciara's voice is like a drone of tinnitus in my ears.

I gave her my passport. My suitcase. My house keys. My car keys. Some clothes. I've made it easy for her to take over my life. The only thing left to take is my husband. Was I so furious with Ryan, that I'd have agreed to anything? *Payback with a difference*, she said.

As the tablets kick in, my mind slows down. The last thought I have before I slip away, is that if it's not money Ciara's after, what is it? She told me, more than once, that she couldn't wait to meet my errant husband.

OMG... is it possible she already knew him? If so, what the hell does she really want?

22

CIARA

Ryan never reappeared last night, after he raced upstairs to check his emails. I waited for over an hour, before I gave up, turned off all the lights, and crept upstairs.

This morning he's just gone out. I'm watching from the spare bedroom window as he walks slowly down the front path, and picks his way over the gravel as if they're hot coals. He crosses the road, and hesitates with his hand on top of the small gate that leads into Olivia and Kenneth's property.

I dive behind the curtain when he glances round, and wait a couple of seconds before I look out again. Ryan inches towards their front door, and holds his finger over the bell before he looks up. The blinds are shut on the two upstairs windows facing onto the street. He'll be wondering if Olivia and Kenneth are still in bed, as both cars are parked out front.

Flo let off steam by telling me about Kenneth spitting in Ryan's face, and yelling abuse for the whole street to hear. Sharing what happened seemed to help Flo. Kenneth yelled for at least ten minutes, and Flo was thrilled when several neighbours came out to see what the fuss was about.

She never went out, but carried on packing her case, and only let rip when Ryan reappeared.

'Were you trying to apologise? Don't fret, Ryan. Kenneth will stay with Olivia. He'll not kick her out, because what woman in her right mind is going to give Kenneth a second look? Well, don't think I'll put up with you, Ryan Bartlam. You can go to hell.'

She repeated this to me several times. It was good to hear her say she wouldn't take him back.

Ryan is now stabbing at the bell. He steps down from the porch, and even from where I'm standing, I can tell he's nervous. He's moving on the spot, like a jogger at traffic lights. He inches back further until his foot hits a flowerpot at the same moment the door cracks open, and Olivia appears.

I assume it's Olivia. She's certainly no match for Flo. Olivia's hair is frizzy, wild. What was Ryan thinking? He must have been very drunk. The thought turns my stomach.

Olivia looks over her shoulder before coming out, and then pulls the door to. She won't want Kenneth to know who is calling. She's wearing a black satin gown thing, and even without binoculars, you can see her enormous breasts straining through the material. She could be a soft porn movie star. Isn't she worried who might be looking?

She leans provocatively against the door, and although I can only see the back of Ryan's head, I guess he's staring at her chest. Again my insides churn.

Ryan is getting agitated, and he's put a threatening arm against the door, blocking her way back inside. He'll be asking about Flo, and no doubt about me. Asking Olivia if she's met me, or knows who I am. He's desperate for answers, and Olivia is his last hope.

As I stare at them, Olivia holds up a hand, as if to say, *Whoa. Get off.*

Ryan grabs her by the wrist, and seems to be losing his cool.

When he puts his face right up close, her gown gapes open and her right breast pops out. Shit.

I can't watch any more. I grab my phone, the car and house keys, and race down the stairs. I need to get out of here before Ryan gets back.

23

CIARA

It's been a long day. This morning after I left the house, I wandered round the shops, treated myself to a couple of flirty tops. Flo said I could wear her clothes, that she didn't mind, and I was excited to look more like her. She's got expensive tastes, loads of designer labels, but jeez, her clothes are so mumsy. I miss my 'tarty gear', as Patrick calls it, and need to sex up the outfits.

Around lunchtime, I came back, but parked the Audi a couple of streets away, and walked up Hillside Gardens until I was standing outside Olivia's front door. I knew Ryan would have been long gone. She opened the door, and after only a couple of random questions, invited me in. I told her I was a friend of Flo's, and thought it would be nice to have a chat. She didn't waste any time flinging the door wide.

She was dressed in 'working-from-home' gear. Sweatpants, baggy jumper, and a flowery headband wrapped round disastrous hair. She obviously wasn't expecting Ryan back.

Her kitchen is pretty much like Flo and Ryan's, designed for entertaining, and drinking. We sat opposite each other at the kitchen bar, and she confided this is where she and Flo regularly sit. I didn't let on I already knew.

I reckon, if I'm going to hang around for a while, I should get to know Olivia better, and make it harder for Flo to knuckle back in if all goes to plan.

Olivia's opening gambit was, 'I really thought I was talking to Flo last night on the phone. You sounded so like her. I thought she was back home.'

She didn't ask why I was using Flo's phone, and when I didn't offer to tell her, she didn't push.

She drinks faster than I do if that's possible. It was as if she hadn't spoken to anyone in days, and she never stopped for breath. I thought the Irish could talk, but Olivia never let up.

I simply told her Flo had invited me to stay for a few days, as she's still not ready to come home. I did let slip about Patrick, though, which made her eyes light up, and gave vent to a whole string of questions.

I've no idea how Flo stands Olivia. All I can imagine is that Flo must get mighty bored. She used to work as a pharmacist, but after getting married, she enjoyed being a lady of leisure.

'I like being a kept woman,' Flo told me. She sounded convincing, but I wonder if she's enjoying her new-found freedom more. I envy the marriage thing, the big house, the dishy husband, regular income, but I couldn't stay at home all day. Ladies' lunches bore me to death.

I listened to an hour's worth of gossip from Olivia, gleaning meaningless titbits about the other neighbours. Although, I was interested to hear about Freddie and Jolie Harden who've got a garden party coming up soon, as I'm after an invite. Olivia doesn't seem to like them, well, certainly not Jolie, and I get the feeling Olivia doesn't like women too much in general. After a brief introduction to her pasty-faced husband, Kenneth, I see why she made a beeline for Ryan. She must be bored to death.

When Olivia began slurring her words, I knew that was my cue to go. I'd been going to ask her to come jogging, but she had enough trouble getting off her stool. Flo never mentioned how overweight she is, or her wobbling double chins.

I spend the next few hours in Starbucks doing crossword puzzles, and devouring a twisty thriller read: *4 Riverside Close*. I'd love to write. Plots swarm like bees in my brain. Gruesome plots, and all things murder.

High on caffeine, it's almost six when I pick up the Audi, and drive back up Hillside Gardens to home. Yes, it's already starting to feel familiar.

I take a few deep breaths, insert the key, and creep as quietly as possible into the house. I'm assuming Ryan is in, but as he keeps his Mercedes convertible in the garage, I can't be sure. Gut instinct tells me he'll not have gone far.

My heart is racing as I take my shoes off, and I'm praying he'll have calmed down since last night. Also, I wonder how his chat with Olivia went this morning. He looked wound up, but at least I know she couldn't have told him anything more about Flo. Olivia had no idea where Flo went, and is none the wiser about when she's coming back.

I wait in the hall, listening for movement. The TV isn't on. There's no sound from upstairs, and you could hear a pin drop, it's like a morgue. I tiptoe past the lounge, do a double take, and back-pedal.

Ryan is draped across the sofa, with a thick tumbler full of whiskey in his hand. I can smell it from here.

'Hi, Ryan.'

He jumps to life as if he's seen a ghost. His default anger isn't slow to rise.

'Where the hell have you been? It's...' he flicks a cuff back, looks at his watch '... six o'clock.'

'Hello to you too. How was your day?' I don't intend to wind him up, but he's such an easy target.

'I've been hanging around all day.'

'Jeez. I'm not your wife. What's up?'

You can tell what's up by just looking at him. Dishevelled is being polite. He looks worse that I imagined possible. But he's still drop-dead gorgeous, and the threatening face does nothing to dampen his handsome features.

'Didn't you get Flo's email last night? I assumed you had, as I didn't see you again.'

'Yes. But I'm none the wiser.' He's now trying to sit up straight, but he's really drunk. I like that we share Irish traits.

'Okay. Let me get myself a drink, and we can put the world to rights. And I'll tell you what you want to know.'

I go to the kitchen, and lift out the bottle of Cloudy Bay from the fridge. I spotted it yesterday on the wine rack. It's one of half a dozen Flo keeps for special occasions.

I unscrew the cap, fearful that it's too early to celebrate. But it tastes so good, and the chilled nectar slips down nicely. I need enough to get me talking, but not enough to spill the beans.

I freeze when I hear Ryan come in. He's followed me, and is now standing right behind me.

24

FLO

The ferry finally pulls away from the quay, as it heads towards the Copeland Islands.

It's Sunday, and there's still been no word from Ciara. Even Ryan has gone quiet. Although I haven't yet responded to his barrage of emails, his silence makes me even more uneasy.

At least my ankle has calmed down, and the painkillers seem to be doing the trick. With everything else on my mind, it's the least of my worries. I've wrapped it tightly with a crepe bandage that Damian managed to locate in the hotel's first-aid kit.

Patrick and I have to sit down as soon as the boat moves off. Five minutes in, the rickety vessel begins to roll from side to side, lurching every few seconds as if it's hit a rock. I cling to the side, expecting the boat to break up, and sink to the bottom of the ocean. The sides of the ferry are so low, that every time the boat tilts, water sloshes onto the deck. Small rubber tyres line each side of the wooden craft to protect it from smashing apart if it ever manages to dock.

Patrick was thrilled when I agreed to come. He's constantly trying to do a sales pitch on County Down. Before I met Ciara, he didn't have to work so hard, but she wedged herself between us and things got awkward. Patrick is great company, and I dared dream of a future together. But I'm no longer sure of anything.

The Copeland Island bird sanctuaries and ancient burial mounds are the last things on my mind. Today, I need Patrick's help, without spilling the beans of exactly what's going on.

I start fiddling with my mobile, slithery fingers flapping like wet fish across the screen. The swaying motion makes purchase difficult.

'Can you try Ciara? I can't get a signal,' I lie, asking Patrick for the third time.

I keep my phone averted from his gaze, but he's not looking. My signal strength is strong, but I need him to call, using his phone. It's the only chance that Ciara might pick up, as she's ignoring all my attempts at communication.

But Patrick's mind is elsewhere. He clutches the side of the rickety vessel with both hands, and his head lolls over the side, putrid green splodges like paint splatters dotting his face. For a coastal dweller, his sea legs are surprisingly shaky. His eyes have lost their sparkle and his cheeks have acquired burgeoning bulges like an overstuffed hamster. But his nose isn't twitching.

'Okay, but can it wait until we get off this bloody thing?' he yells. His voice booms like a foghorn but the words dissipate into thin air, as the waves buffet the vessel.

My phone gets even harder to keep hold of, as sea spume sprays everywhere. Patrick stretches out a hand, takes it off me, and slips it into his pocket.

'Wait till we get off. You don't want the feckin' thing falling overboard.'

My fingers are white, and so stiff that I can't bend the joints. Patrick claps his hands like seal flippers on top of mine, to shock them back to life.

'I told you to wear gloves.' His yell softens as it reaches my ears, then swooshes past. I'm impressed by his concern as his green pouches quiver, and his Adam's apple bobs up and down when he swallows.

The Northern Ireland weather has tricked us. Again. The morning decoy of bright sunshine and clear skies had given way to drizzle by the time we reached Donaghadee to board the ferry. When we clambered aboard the rocking death trap, for what was supposed to be a pleasant sightseeing trip, a dank grey roof had settled overhead. Suddenly, it was as if someone pulled a trigger, and let rip a ricochet of sodden bullets.

We chug into Chapel Bay on Copeland Island, and drop anchor. I check my watch again. We've only been at sea for twenty-five minutes, and I'm desperate to get my phone back.

Stepping onto dry land couldn't feel any better, and Patrick's smile returns once we've staggered ashore. In an instant, he livens up. He sweeps his arm round the bay to ignite my enthusiasm, and prods me in the ribs.

'Isn't it amazing? Just look at that view.'

Damp clings to me, and my clothes are wet through. I sneeze three times in quick succession.

'Yes. It's amazing,' I chirp, not wanting to dampen his spirits, but the view is dismal.

Maybe it's my general mood that sours my thoughts, but the ruins of a church and burial ground, ancient as hell, make jumping up and down hard to do. I wonder at Patrick's enthusiasm, but I suspect firm ground is feeding his exuberance, as it quickly steadies the sea legs. *You're a cynic, that's your problem.* Ryan's in my head.

'Fantastic, isn't it?' Patrick repeats, desperate for me to agree. He needs me to share his passions, to feed him hope of a future together. I know I'd feel differently if my mind wasn't all over the place. Patrick deserves better.

Hie eyes scan the shoreline, the landscape pitted with desolate salt marshes and wet grasslands. He points to the right.

'Look over there. Puffins. On those rocks. Can't you see their black and white underpants?' Patrick laughs, takes my hand and stretches my arm in their direction. His eyes are ablaze with excitement. 'They're a rare sight,' he says.

I so can't concentrate. Instead, I ask Patrick for my phone back, rubbing damp palms along my jeans. I sound like a spoilt child, asking again and again, pretending I can't get connection.

'Sorry, but I want to see if I've got a signal yet.'

It's not really my phone I want to look at. I'm desperate for Patrick to dig out his mobile, which is usually stuck to his fingers.

Every day when he jogs along the beach, he grips his phone in one hand, and a water bottle in the other. But since we left this morning, his phone has been strangely out of sight. Perhaps in deference to my quips about mobile phones, security blankets and thumb sucking.

I think I'm being unfair, because he told me today's outing was his treat, so maybe that's why he's keeping his mobile zipped away, not to spoil the occasion. Just the two of us. A shiver shoots through my body, and makes me wonder at his definition of treat.

'Have you got a signal on your phone?' I ask, as we head away from the boat which rocks vigorously in the bay. I pray it will still be in one piece when we want to head back.

We trudge, as if on a death march, with squawking gulls for company.

Get your bloody phone out. Why is he ignoring me? Patrick is trying to look smug. *See. I don't always have my phone on.* That's his mood. It's a male one-upmanship thing. I try not to look uneasy but I'm panicky as hell, on high alert while trying to look relaxed, and in tune with nature. It's not easy.

Up ahead, a kestrel suddenly parts a flock of gulls which is perched on a rocky cliff top. The mighty bird of prey swoops down, scattering the chipper group with a vicious slice of its mammoth wingspan.

'Did you see that?' Patrick's hand dips into his jacket and he finally produces my phone. I grab it, tap at the screen, but the battery is really dead.

'Shit, I forgot to charge it,' I say turning the screen towards him. I don't tell him I deliberately didn't charge it. I need him to make the call.

'Can you try Ciara for me on yours? Please. I need to check everything's okay.'

I still haven't told Patrick anything about Ciara's and my ploy. Nor the photos and videos she sent me. All Patrick knows is that she's spending a few days in London, in my house. Sleeping under the same roof as my husband.

'You still haven't spoken to her? Here. I'll give her a call,' Patrick says.

I'm not sure if he's surprised I still haven't spoken to Ciara, or if he's deliberately being flippant.

Whichever it is, he's in no hurry to make the call.

25

FLO

The kestrel circles, eager for death meat, and swoops in for the kill. I've an eerie sense of how it feels.

Patrick scrolls down recent calls. I have the most dreadful urge to snatch the phone off him. He's so relaxed, too relaxed, as if he's deliberately toying with me by taking so long. When he finally puts the phone to his ear, my body stiffens. I can't move.

'Ciara? Is that you? How are you?' A second passes. 'Patrick. Who the hell do you think it is?'

Before he can finish his sentence, I make a grab for the phone. Patrick tuts, rolls his eyes, and holds his hands up in surrender.

I clamp the phone to my ear, and march ahead. Before speaking, I tune in for background noises. For any sound, no matter how small, or insignificant. I listen for clues. The kettle whistling in the background, or Ryan's irritated voice as it comes to the boil.

'Why can't we have an electric kettle like everyone else?' Ryan asks the same question daily. He's not patient. He mocks I must have too much free time if I can hang around for the whistling kettle.

'I don't want to be like everyone else. Anyway, the whistle is comforting.'

I don't know why I'm listening for the kettle. If Ryan is around, I'd most likely hear his angry voice. Especially if Ciara is on the phone. He'll be freaking out.

But there's no background noise. It's as if Ciara is in an empty room, as there's only a faint echo as if off bare walls, but nothing else.

'Ciara. Can you hear me? What the hell is going on?' There's a faint intake of breath. It could me mine, I'm not sure, but instantly the phone goes dead. 'Ciara? Ciara? Are you there?'

I yell into the handset, spitting out the words. The bitch has hung up.

'Shit. Shit. Shit. She hung up on me.' I stomp my feet, before letting out an almighty scream. Patrick looks on helplessly.

'Listen. The signal's not good, she probably got cut off. Don't worry, she'll get back,' he says.

'I doubt it.'

'Here. Let's take a selfie and send her that.'

A selfie? He's got to be kidding me.

But Patrick isn't worried, not a flicker of concern. He really has no idea of what's going on, which gives me small comfort. If he does know more than he's letting on, he's hiding it well. Perhaps his easy manner, winsome smile, is all an act. It could be Irish blarney, as I don't know who to trust.

Patrick's green cheeks are now ruddy, and glowing with all the fresh air. His black hair is tossed all over the place, swirling round his head like dirty candy floss. It's spun in wiry strands, and for the first time I notice a faint thinning patch on top.

He takes his phone, pulls me close, and stretches an arm out in front to take the selfie. I can't unlock my gritting teeth, but Patrick beams, presenting top and bottom rows of teeth.

I manage a vague tilt of my lips, but it's more snarl than smile. My eyes blaze through hooded lids. It's the most menacing I can muster.

Once Patrick has taken the shot, I start up again. Dog with a bone.

'Send it now. Go on.' I'm now jiggling on the spot again. 'Add a message and ask her to call you back. Please. And...'

Patrick gets to work.

'And? What else do I need to add?'

He's so damn relaxed.

'Ask her how Ryan is taking her visit.'

He doesn't ask what I mean, but then I haven't told him Ryan had no idea she would be turning up.

'Happy now? It's all sent. Now let's have some fun.' He zips his phone away. 'And can we please forget about Ciara. There's so much to see.'

When he takes my hand, links our fingers together, it feels good. He pulls me along in his long stride, and chuckles when I can't keep up. I did show him my bandaged ankle earlier, telling him I'd tripped over a loose paving slab, but I don't want to spoil the moment by complaining about the dull ache. Patrick is so happy.

He's now on a mission to cover as much ground as possible. Also, I suspect he's trying to stop me talking.

And who could blame him?

26

FLO

We traipse round the island in silence. Patrick doesn't do silence as a rule.

Perhaps the wind and weather have zapped his energy, but I feel he's deliberately holding his tongue.

Not long after we met, he asked me question after question.

Where did you meet Ryan? How did you know he was the one? What happened? Who was Olivia?

Patrick is nothing if not persistent. He digs like an archaeologist up against stubborn rock. The more stubborn, the more he chisels away. But he's gone quiet, eerily quiet, and the bleakness of the landscape isn't helping.

We follow the cliff path that skirts the island, trudging across the bracken-strewn undergrowth. My ears prick up, my senses on high alert, for when he finally speaks. It's not about Ciara, or about us. Rather, he tries to ignite my damp enthusiasm with a potted history of the island. His voice is assured, like a schoolmaster's, and I find myself getting sucked into the lesson.

We pass the site of an early school, nineteenth century, where twenty-eight pupils were taught: kids of one hundred inhabitants.

Patrick then turns to wildlife, and reels off lists of rare birds that mark out the territory. He's so keen to suck me in, I stop in my tracks, put a hand across his mouth, before I kiss him.

His lips are full, but freezing cold.

'What's that for?' He pulls me close, wraps me up inside his coat.

'To say thanks. And...'

'Not another "and". What now?' he says. His worried look comes back. Furrowed brow, droopy mouth.

'We need to be getting back, don't we? The boat leaves in twenty minutes.'

'Christ. I'd forgotten the time. Come on. Race you back.'

As he races ahead, I realise I could fall for Patrick. Even more than I have already.

* * *

The ferry journey back to Donaghadee is even worse than coming out. Passengers are packed like sardines into the buffeting crate.

'Where have all these people come from?' I ask Patrick.

Before he has a chance to answer, the boat is moving off. A couple of minutes and it's already rolling from side to side. Patrick re-cements his hands onto the boat rail, and braces himself. He closes his eyes, struggles to breathe, and from his hunched shoulders I think he's about to heave overboard.

Instead, he manages somehow to get out his mobile, and turns the screen towards me.

'Look. Ciara liked the picture. She's posted it on Instagram.'

I take the phone, check out the post. She's written 'All at Sea' across the image. Bitch. She's taunting us. And I know it's aimed at me.

'Call her again. Please, Patrick. You've got a good signal.' I could be asking him to make a life-or-death 999 call, I'm so desperate. I bite my lip, and taste the tang of blood.

'Let's sit down. I'm feeling pretty rough. Can it wait till we get off?'

'Give it to me. I can try it. Please?'

Patrick rings her number, and passes me the phone. I've no idea what I'll say. Patrick is so close. But I needn't have worried, as it goes to messaging.

'She's not picking up.'

'Leave her a message then.' Patrick is fed up with me. I reluctantly pass him back the phone.

'There's no point. Your battery is pretty low now too.'

'Come here. Why don't you call Ryan if you're that worried?'

It's a good question. But what would I tell him? That I invited Ciara into our home because we had concocted a plan to irritate and humiliate him. That I asked her to take my place for a few days while I decide whether to give him a second chance. Or leave him for good.

Or would I tell him that I have evidence of him committing cold-blooded murder, and the woman in our home told me not to contact him. I've no idea what Ciara is planning, but I'm scared to go behind her back. Just in case.

'It's okay. I can call Ryan later. No worries.'

'Are you still really mad at Ryan? Is that why you won't phone him?'

'Something like that,' I say.

Patrick seems relieved, and brushes salty lips against mine. He's starting to look pretty rough again, his face already tinged with green. His strong arm, which was wrapped round my waist, flails as the boat heaves.

Patrick turns his head and looks longingly towards the shore. I watch him, and wonder. Perhaps it's my heightened senses, my increasing paranoia, but I have the oddest feeling that Patrick is hiding something. I can't put my finger on it, but again it's female intuition.

We finally reach the harbour, and Patrick brightens up. Once the gangplank is in place, he leads the way. I bypass his outstretched arm, and confidently walk the short distance.

On the drive back to Ballyholme, neither of us says much. Patrick keeps his eyes on the road, and I try to stay awake. The sea air has sapped our energy.

As my eyes begin to shut, I feel the swaying motion of the ferry, and my head spins.

It's as if I'm about to fall overboard.

27

CIARA

'Where have you been all day?' Ryan slurs the question, but he's so drunk, he's having trouble getting anything out.

'I popped in to see Olivia.' It's too tempting not to tell him. 'Jeez. She can drink.'

'What? Is that where you've been? All this time?' He looks confused, as if he's not sure whether to blow his top, or carry on asking questions.

'Look, I'll make some coffee, and I'll tell you what you want to know.'

I'll tell him some of it, the bits I want him to know, but he needs to sober up first.

He swills the last of the whiskey round in his glass, knocks it back, and hands me the glass.

He's even drunker than I thought because he stumbles trying to sit down. As I fire up the Nespresso machine, Ryan stares mutely ahead.

I unpeel my jumper, and throw it down. My T-shirt hangs off one shoulder, and gapes if I lift my arms up. Not wearing a bra is a ploy, but I'm not sure in his drunken state Ryan will notice.

'Sugar? Two, I think Flo told me.' I set down the double-shot espresso, and a small bowl of sugar lumps.

He pops one in the coffee, and stirs so vigorously, coffee spits over the side.

'Right. Let's start at the beginning,' he says. 'What's your name?'

'Ciara. Ciara McCluskey.'

'Why are you here?' He knocks back the coffee, and asks for a refill.

'Coming up. Why am I here? Because Flo invited me to stay for a few days while she decided what to do.'

'Where is she? Decided what to do about what?'

He's sobering up pretty quickly, as his tone is already snappier.

'About everything. I'm sorry, but she's met someone else, Ryan.' I fiddle with the coffee pods, and there's a moment of eerie silence.

'Go on.'

'His name's Patrick. An Irish guy.'

'You're Irish. Shit. I knew you had an accent. You're bloody Irish.' He knocks back the second espresso, coughs, and sits up much straighter. He taps his fingers on the table.

'I met Flo in Bangor,' I said.

'Bangor? You're kidding me. She swore she'd never go back there. What's she doing in Bangor?'

'Ballyholme, to be precise,' I say. He hasn't twigged, or made any connections yet. I'll not be joining up the dots for him, not till I've had some fun.

'What is it you want? Why are you here?'

'Flo and I met in a pub, and we sort of hit it off. Your wife likes her wine, doesn't she?'

I flinch at the word 'wife'. 'She'd easily pass the Irish drinking test.' I force a laugh.

'Flo wouldn't invite a complete stranger into our house. Not without telling me first.' Ryan's voice has got louder, as he tries to convince himself of what he's saying. I'm surprised he's not more interested in Patrick, but I suspect he's not used to competition.

'Flo told me you'd been there together.'

'Where?'

'Bangor.' He's still looking pretty blank. Nothing. 'I hear your mother was from Ballyholme.'

You could hear a pin drop. He starts to click his knuckles, before linking his fingers behind his head. He seems to have a 'eureka' moment, because he slams his hands down so hard that his cup jumps up. He leans his face towards me, stretches his neck like a turtle.

'Why can't I get hold of Flo? She warned me not to go to the police. Why the hell would I go to the police if she asked you to stay?'

'We're just having a bit of fun.'

It's a bit more than fun, but it's up to him to work it out.

'Flo and I became good friends. She was pretty upset when I first met her, and told me what a naughty boy you'd been.' I fiddle with the gold cross around my neck, and Ryan's eyes wander, as I stick my chest out. The T-shirt is loose, and leaves nothing to the imagination. 'Anyway, we thought it would be a bit of fun, if I turned up and took over wifely duties for a while.'

'Is that it?' He puffs out a relief of whiskey breath.

'Also I've never been to London, so it seemed like a plan. Kill two birds, and all that.'

'Listen. If you give me Flo's new number, I'll talk to her. If it's only for a few days, and she's happy with it, then perhaps you can stay. Only a few days mind.'

Ryan gets up, pushes his chair roughly under the table, and takes his empty coffee cup over to the sink. He stands for ages staring out at the back garden. I wonder if he's shocked by his appearance in the long expanse of window. I would be if I were him. His chin is coated in uneven stubble, and his hair looks in shock, sticking out all over the place.

He lifts a damp cloth, and swishes it across the dust-speckled glass to get a better look. Could be of the garden, but I'd guess it's of himself. I wander up behind him, and he doesn't budge, but he's seen me.

'We'll make it work. A few days only. If I play my cards right, perhaps you'll let me stay longer,' I whisper in his ear, then I push my breasts into his back, and circle his waist with my arms.

It takes a second. Maybe two, three, before he reacts.

'What the fuck? Get off me.' He's aiming for furious, but there's a lack of bite.

He swings round, clamps his hands against my shoulders, and thrusts me backwards.

'Woah. I was only being friendly.' I hold my hands up in surrender, turn away and let my bare feet suck across the icy tiles.

I feel his eyes on my back, following me. I wiggle my hips, my tight skirt shimmying up near my thighs, and pause by the kitchen door. I trill my fingers over my shoulder.

'Night, Ryan. See you tomorrow.'

And with that, I walk slowly into the hall, and on up the stairs.

28

CIARA

The spare bed is so uncomfortable. Sleep is like a pipe dream, impossible.

Ryan has long since gone to bed. I heard him, when I went to the toilet, whistling in his sleep. Every time I close my eyes, I can't switch off. It's hard not to feel bitter, when I compare my upbringing to Flo's. Things came easily to her, but I've had to fight for everything.

It all started in Bantry Bay. In all weathers, I perched like a leprechaun, cross-legged on one of the metal bollards that lined the port. Thick rope circled my post like a hangman's noose.

I would lay Grandpa's flat cap on the ground and fill it with small change that glinted in the sunlight. But my begging bowl only increased the hunger in my soul, and my discontent. I was jealous of the sassy travellers who tripped off cruise ships and tossed loose change at the welcoming curio. I wanted to swap places, be like them. I've been striving ever since.

The English held the greatest interest. The mainland wasn't far away, within touching distance. Stressed executives came with bulging wallets. They'd fly into Cork, speed through the country lanes in flashy hire cars, and invade our province like aliens from outer space.

The weekend trippers headed straight for the packed pubs, and got drunk on Guinness and Irish music. With their stylish luggage and expensive clothes, they partied like prisoners out on bail. They also had a penchant for wild and wanton Irish women.

I grew up in a family of bigots and religious zealots. And, of course, alcoholics. The way of life is as deeply etched into our psyches as the epitaphs on the headstones in the Abbey Cemetery which lies just around the corner.

Mummy still lives in Bantry, and moans daily about her birthplace. Why she never tried to leave, I've no idea. Not even after the nuns condemned her to purgatory for a debauched moment of madness, and gave birth to a bastard child. But she still goes to church on a Sunday to ask forgiveness and pray for salvation.

I couldn't get away fast enough from the godforsaken hole. I also go to church, and pray. Mummy is doing her best, her penance being to help me out.

The rugged majesty of the south-west of Ireland might one day call me back, when I'm ready to embrace its powerful splendour. But for now, it's time to take what I've always wanted. What I've earned. A better life.

Albeit another person's life.

29

CIARA

I managed to avoid Ryan all day yesterday, giving him time to calm down after our heated conversation.

I headed up London, and did a bit of sightseeing, taking a trip on the London Eye, and visiting the Tower of London. When I got back, I crept up to my room, and read. Ryan made even less noise than I did, as I fell asleep early and didn't hear him come upstairs.

This morning, I wait until he's left for work before I get up. My plan is to catch up with him today over lunch. Even though Flo says he doesn't like surprises, I'll take my chances.

I mooch around the master bedroom, and tug open the doors to Flo's wardrobe. It's on the right, Ryan's is on the left. Flo's got a weird obsessive thing about the right. Like the number eight. She's got a long list of superstitious habits. Me... I love ducking under a ladder, booking a room on the thirteenth floor. I'm hoping Ryan will like the contrast.

Flo's wardrobe is meticulously ordered. I swoosh hangers from side to side, lingering when something fancy catches my eye. My fingers caress the pure cotton and silken fabrics.

Her clothes are arranged like folders in a filing system. They're that neatly hung, everything displayed inside see-through covers. I lift pieces out to admire, like in a high-end couturier. Even track-suit bottoms are systematically arranged alongside torn designer jeans. Casual tops, dressy blouses, light sweaters, and cardigans have their own separate section. My hand comes to rest at the smart work outfits, although I'd like to spend more time browsing the sexy party clothes. They'll have to wait for another time, although a quick glance doesn't scream sexy. Stylish, classy, but a man would need a bloody good imagination.

I lift out a chic navy and white dress, and hold it up against my body, swivelling round to face the long free-standing mirror. I tilt my head this way and that before I unzip the content and take it out. When I slip the dress on, I'm surprised how good it looks. It fits like a glove.

Flo's shoes are in a separate cubicle in the spare room where I'm sleeping. Sleeping for now, at any rate. I don't plan on staying in the cramped space. The master bedroom is much more appealing, with Ryan being the main attraction.

Pairs of shoes are crammed into the cubicle. Neat piles of shoe-boxes, with picture labels on the ends showing what's inside, are like contents of a shoe store.

You can tell Flo doesn't go to work, as there is a dearth of sensible pairs. Fancy pumps, skyscraper stilettos and kitten heels are on a top shelf, with only a couple of pairs of trainers and flat-ties on the bottom. I count thirty-eight pairs of footwear, and this doesn't include the six pairs of boots downstairs.

Hunkering on the floor, I check out the navy shoe options. Like Cinderella, I slip on the suede kitten heels with sling-backs. It's fun wandering up and down the red bedroom carpet. Flo's feet are slightly smaller than mine, but no sweat. I adjust the sling-backs to a more generous setting.

In the master bedroom are two drawers of accessories. The

contents read like another chapter in Flo's autobiography, although I'm surprised by the strings of pearls. Flo certainly flew light to Ireland, no sign of frippery, glamour, mascara, or eyeshadow. Lip gloss has been her only daily effort. When I met her, her wan, pasty appearance spurred me on, as I make much more of an effort in the looks department.

I finger through the jewellery, and start to fill in the colours on my paint-by-number image of Ryan's wife. I make a mental note of the detail, things that Ryan might like, and try to work out his tastes.

Flo's jewellery collection oozes expense. Gold-linked chains, diamond-studded earrings, vintage brooches, and charms. Guilt presents perhaps? It's hard to imagine Flo choosing many of the assorted pieces herself. I'm pretty sure there's more than a hint of male guilt behind the glitzy collection.

I lift out a solid gold neckband, from which dangles a small delicate heart, and clasp it round my throat. I unpin my miniscule ear studs, and replace them with thick knotted gold hoops that match the choker.

Once I'm happy with my choices, I hang everything else back in the wardrobes, and skip downstairs. I've the final piece of my outfit to pick up. The cream loose-fitting Ted Baker coat, summer heaven, hangs on a peg downstairs. I've tried it on more than once since I arrived.

When I'm ready to leave the house, I stop by the hall table and lift a silver-framed photo of Flo and Ryan, the pair all smiles and cloying intimacy. The picture will soon be dispatched under the stairs with the skiing photo. For now, I turn it upside down.

I lock up and set off on the twenty-minute walk to the Tube station. It's almost 11.30, plenty of time to get there by lunchtime. According to Flo, Ryan sticks rigidly to routine. He pops out every day, around one o'clock, for a sandwich. Occasionally to a restaurant near his office.

'You'd never catch Ryan eating at his desk. He takes a full hour for lunch. To be honest, he's more interested in food than work.' Flo was sarcastic, and despite an attempt at humour, she painted a rather drab portrait of Ryan. 'He's irritatingly set in his ways,' she said, eyes rolling upwards. I wonder if she always felt this way, but suspect his infidelity has made her judge him more harshly.

Flo's jibes at Ryan certainly soothe the rough edges of my flimsy guilt. Although her fault-finding was fed by hurt and anger, it helped suck her into my ideas for a payback plan. She had absolutely no idea that it was about anything more than payback for a one-night stand. A *#MeToo* moment for the girls.

Sympathy, and an understanding ear, did the trick. Flo likes to talk, get things off her chest. When she asked me if I thought she'd done the right thing by storming out, I certainly wasn't going to disagree.

'Exactly the right thing. What a bastard,' I told her.

30

CIARA

The Tube train rumbles along. I lick a tissue, swish it across the filthy window to get a better look. My dark eyebrows look startled, and my eyes don't look much better.

The cream-coloured Ted Baker coat is already slightly crumpled, and when I sniff at a sleeve, there's already the smell of stale carriage. The stifling claustrophobia is a far cry from Bantry where folk walk or ride bikes to work, and chat to passers-by. When the guy across the aisle smiles, I grip my handbag tighter.

When the Tube reaches my stop, I follow the exit signs, climb a few sets of stairs, until I reach civilisation. Fresh air, and the honk of horns, welcome me into the sunlight. I recheck directions, and turn right.

I follow Google Maps. First right, third left, and stride purposefully for the last few yards. The glass-fronted offices of Stauntons, Financial Services, appear in front of me. They look mighty different from online images, that's for sure. The internet threw up a detailed description of a turn-of-the-century building, deceiving the online surfer with expensive images. I doubt if I'd half a million in the bank I'd seek their advice.

A glance through the windows, and the bijou reception tells me I'd likely have gone elsewhere. Ryan's backstreet offices are nothing like the online collages. A last check of my appearance in the shiny glass entrance, and I pull back the thick steel handles.

I secure Flo's Mulberry handbag across a bent arm, and flick back a straggling fringe. I can't wait to see if members of staff twig that I'm not Ryan's wife.

When I reach the reception desk, a pink-cheeked girl with blonde curls, looks up.

'Good morning, Mrs Bartlam.'

'Good morning, Chloe. Would you let Mr Bartlam know I'm here please.'

She clicks a few buttons on her phone, announces my arrival, and no more than two minutes pass before I see Ryan overhead slide across a shiny floor as if he's ice-skating.

He manages to slow when he reaches the iron railing at the top of the short flight of stairs, but his smooth-grained brown leather brogues teeter over the top step, as if he's on a cliff edge.

I smile, trill my fingers. OMG. He really was expecting Flo.

My kitten heels click across the polished floor, and even from this distance, I see Ryan's knuckles whiten. He's gripping the metal banister as if it's life or death.

'Hi.' I look up, inch back the generous coat sleeve, and point at my watch. Okay, so it's one of Flo's fancy watches. 'Wondered if you fancied lunch? I've just finished shopping.'

He looks in shock, and a lack of shopping bags is the last thing on his mind.

A work colleague comes up behind him, nudges past, and mumbles something. The young guy smiles at me.

'Hi,' he says, hesitating a second, before he walks on.

Ryan must have slid down the handrail because he's suddenly standing in front of me.

'What the hell are you doing here?' he hisses in a loud whisper, looking round the empty foyer as he does so.

'Ouch. That hurts,' I squeal, not so quietly, when he grabs my arm. He crunches his spare hand into the small of my back, and orders me to keep moving.

I feel like a hostage with a gun in my back. Chloe lowers her eyes, fiddles with non-existent papers, as we pass.

'Where did you get that coat? It's Flo's, isn't it?' Ryan's voice gets louder as he thrusts me towards the exit. He tugs at a handle and, with his other hand, circles my wrist before catapulting me onto the street.

'*Get-off-me-now!*' I let rip, slapping his arm away. No idea why he thinks he's calling the shots.

'What the fuck are you doing here?' His voice slows down, as he tries to rein in the aggression. 'Well?' He moves away from me once we're outside.

I have to swallow my own anger, and it takes a second to simmer down.

'What's all the fuss about? I was curious to see where you worked, and thought I could treat you to lunch. Say thanks.'

I have to turn my face away from the intensity of his stare. He struts ahead, muttering under his breath. He's good at muffled obscenities, it's quite an art form, because he knows right well that he's been heard.

As more staff filter out from his offices, he walks even faster. Flo's kitten heels are a snug fit, but they're hard to jog in. I turn my ankle, hop up and down in pain.

'Can't you just slow down,' I yell.

He turns, looks down at my ankle. If he recognises Flo's shoes, he doesn't comment. He stuffs his hands in his pockets.

'Are you okay?' he asks. He grits his teeth when I overdo the hobbling.

'I'll live.'

When I do catch up with him, we're standing outside a small pizzeria.

'This any good?' I run a finger down an outside menu. 'It looks nice.'

'The pizzas are good,' he says, hands back in his pockets. Not sure if he's trying to resist the urge to punch me, or if he's calmed down.

'Let's go in here then.'

He extracts his hands, slides a shaky finger between his neck and collar, and yanks his pink tie to one side, undoing a top button in the process.

'After you,' he says, and tugs the door.

I look down at my ankle, and stumble against him in the small space. I feel him stiffen, but he says nothing.

31

CIARA

The pizzeria is noisy. A waiter with a goatee beard, and a nose ring, leads us to a table in the corner.

'Is this okay, Mr Bartlam?'

'Fine, thanks.' Ryan presses something into the guy's hand, and pats him on the back.

The waiter smiles at me, and sort of does a double take.

'Madam,' he says, pulling out a chair. I wonder if he thinks I'm Mrs Bartlam. The icy atmosphere between Ryan and I would suggest I'm the wife, and that we've had an argument.

'Thanks,' I say with a broad smile, as I slip off Flo's coat.

I want to ask Ryan if Flo's been here, but I know when to hold my tongue. He slumps heavily into his seat.

'Can I get you any drinks?' The waiter hovers, an off-white cloth draped across an arm. It looks as if it's been wiping dirty dishes.

Ryan nods at a suggestion of a carafe of house red, and we sit in silence until the waiter has gone.

Ryan then seems to wake up. Think disturbed rattlesnake.

'You know what?' he asks.

I lift a serviette from a holder, and roll it tight in my fingers.

'What do I know?'

He looks as if he's about to explode.

'I've had enough of this bloody charade. If you have to stay for a few days, I don't want to be involved. Do-you-get-it?'

'Loud and clear. Christ, keep your hair on.'

Ryan lifts a cardboard menu and flaps it up and down in front of his face.

This time, I'm the one to lean across.

'I just want to say thank you. Is that so bad? Flo will be back soon enough.'

His eyes light up. Think little boy on Christmas morning.

'You know when Flo's coming back? Has she told you? When?'

The waiter reappears like Aladdin's genie, and fills our glasses. Ryan's hand wobbles as he lifts his drink, and coughs after the first mouthful.

'Cheers,' I say, but he ignores my outstretched glass.

'When is she coming back?' He's now starting to sound like a stuck record.

'Stop worrying. You'll be the first to know.' Although I doubt that very much.

Even in the half-light of the dingy restaurant, I notice black rings under Ryan's eyes. His lips are dry, soaking up the red tannins from the wine, and his skin is seriously dried out. Wrinkles on his forehead could do with ironing.

'She'll be back when she's ready. But hey. I'm a good listener, why don't you let me have your side of the story.' My smile eggs him on, and I dare place a hand on top of his.

He doesn't snap, just slowly recoils his hand and puts it on his lap.

'It's all such a bloody mess.'

'Go on.'

'I had a stupid one-night stand with Olivia, and it's ruined my life. It was all Olivia's fault, and I was drunk. I don't know how to put it right with Flo. It was a bloody stupid mistake.' His eyes cloud over.

I must say, he's a master at passing the buck. Gulps of wine fuel his accusations. Olivia doesn't come off too well, that's for sure. *Frustrated. Slut. Gagging for it. Prick tease.* Another time, another place, I'd have chucked wine in his face.

Despite what I feel for Ryan, his justifications for shagging his neighbour are hard to stomach. But I'm a good listener, a huge sympathetic ear. Ryan might be a cold-blooded murderer, but I let him talk. Unchallenged, he visibly unwinds. I wince when he cracks his knuckles, it's a really bad habit, but it seems to help his flow.

By the time we've finished our pizzas, he's like a new man. Confessing, without challenge, seems to have done the trick. Confessing to a priest might also have helped, but I can't imagine a priest sticking to a vow of silence if he heard the extent of Ryan's crimes.

I know how it works in the Catholic Church. I've confessed plenty of times, and from the way Ryan talks, I suspect his mother dragged him regularly to the confessional booth.

After he pays the bill, it's his turn to put a hand on top of mine.

'Thanks for listening. Sorry for being such an arse.'

'My pleasure.'

It feels like I've won the lottery. We get up and, with my cheeks aflame, we make our way outside. For a moment it's hard to see, it's so bright.

'Thanks again, Ciara. I mean it. I needed to talk to someone.'

He leans in and kisses me on the cheek. He lingers. I wonder if he recognises Flo's perfume. Midnight. He bought it for her last Christmas. But I don't think his mind is on Flo right at this minute.

Isn't love fickle?

* * *

On the Tube back, I ease into the rocky motion.

This time, I circle a smiley face with my finger on the smeary window, and slot my reflection inside. It smiles back. I look around the half-empty carriage before digging into Flo's Mulberry bag. *The Girl on the Train*. That's me. I unclip the metal tag on the small can of emergency white wine, and toast my success.

Ryan thanked me, not once. Several times. By the time I headed off, he definitely felt better, and so did I.

We're both from good old Catholic Irish stock. Three Hail Marys and all is forgiven.

'My pleasure,' I mouth at myself in the glass. 'You're welcome.'

Now, it's only a matter of time.

32

FLO

After we get back from Donaghadee, I wave Patrick off when he drops me outside the guest house. I tell him I fancy a lie down after all the sea air and excitement. But as soon his car is out of sight, I turn right and head for the centre of town.

Bangor High Street runs from the rocky shoreline at one end, to a roundabout at the top. That's all there is to the town. One long street. It's like a wind tunnel, funnelling salty sea air up its length.

I peer into souvenir shops crammed with harps, Guinness mugs and leprechauns. They're tucked between building societies, banks, and the local butcher's. Up ahead I spot the bright orange sign swinging like a welcoming flag at a fete. *Kennedys Estate Agents*.

The window is plastered with uninviting properties for sale, and when I push open the door, a bell tinkles a tinny welcome.

'Good afternoon.' I hear the greeting before I see the guy. The estate agent is hiding behind a pile of papers on his desk, and when he gets up, his broad easy smile makes me suspect he's counting commissions. I forget for a moment I'm in Ireland, and it's default behaviour.

'How can I help you?' he asks.

'Hi. Mulberry Lodge Nursing Home. I'm after some information. I see it's up for sale.'

'No problem. I'm Rowan, by the way. Have a seat and I'll dig out what we've got.'

Rowan's ruddy complexion clashes with a chunk of orange hair, and his head is so round, it reminds me of a Belisha beacon.

He slides out from behind his desk, and asks if I'd like a coffee.

'Yes please. Milk, two sugars. Thanks.'

As soon as he's gone to the back of the shop, I check my phone. The ten minute ritual has been reduced to every five minutes. When Patrick drove off, I started up again. Each time I see the blank screen, I want to scream; hurl the phone, jump up and down on it. Anything to vent my fury.

Ciara is ghosting me, by phone and by email. She's even stopped posting on Facebook and Twitter, and there's been nothing on Instagram since the 'All at Sea' post. For a social media junkie, it's weird. The lack of showcased selfies makes things worse, as it doesn't make sense. What the heck is she doing? I can't work her out. If she's aiming on blackmail, what's she waiting for?

My mind is buzzing, but the sea air and trudge round the island have depleted my energy reserves. I roar a yawn as Rowan appears with coffees, and hands me a stapled set of papers.

'Thanks. Can I ask you a few questions about the home?' I say, flicking through the printout.

'Fire away.'

When did the home close? Why? Where did the residents go? Who ran the home? Where did the staff go? Who were the staff? Names, ages, gender? Appearances?

Okay, I leave out the last two, but if Rowan was expecting questions as to soundness of structure, subsidence, foundations, and flimsy stud walls, he's pretty cool. He seems glad of the company.

'Staff? My aunt lived there for a while. Dementia patients mainly. I remember a few nurses working shifts,' he says. As he talks, he flicks through a file of papers, and uses a thick tongue to moisten a freckly thumb every couple of sheets. 'Here,' he says, pulling out a newspaper article. 'It seems the home closed after complaints as to hygiene, and the running of the place. As well as a couple of suspicious deaths.'

My stomach lurches. 'And?' I will him to carry on.

'Mr Connor was the manager back then, but he's long retired. There's a photo here of him with the staff.' He swivels round a black and white image.

'When was this taken?' I turn the picture towards the light.

A fan heater whirrs around Rowan's feet, and the hot air smacks me in the face on each rotation. I pull my seat back, but it doesn't help. Perspiration gathers on my hairline, round my neck. I take out a tissue, dab at the dampness, but my cheeks sizzle.

Ciara, despite the starched white cap, stands out. There's no doubt it's her. She's bunched up beside the manager, a flirtatious smile playing for the camera. Mr Connor's arm is wrapped round her waist, their shoulders locked in photo-shoot intimacy.

'About six or seven years ago. Yes, the date's there.' He stubs a finger on the page.

'Any idea who that is?' I ask, voice husky, throat parched.

'Oh, that's Mary. Mary McCluskey. Everyone knows Mary. She's a regular at the bar next door.'

'Mary? Are you sure?'

'Certain. Although she changed her name recently, I hear. God knows why. To Caitlin, or something like that. Cath? No idea why, but she was always a bit strange. Ideas above her station if you ask me. Why? Do you know her?'

'Ciara. That's her name now.'

'Ciara. Yes, that's it.' Rowan flops back in his seat, pushes his pen to the side, as if he's just finished an exam paper.

'Could I hold on to this information? I'm looking at the property for a client.'

Rowan sits up, whiff of a sale, crunches up his plastic cup and chucks it in a bin.

'I can copy it for you. Let me have your email, and I'll keep you posted on any developments.' His eyes widen.

'Sounds good.' I scribble my email on a Post-it note.

'Anything else you're interested in?' he asks, heading for the copier.

'No. Mulberry Lodge. That's all.'

33

FLO

I stayed in bed most of yesterday, wrecked by fresh air and everything that's going on.

My eyes are dried out from looking at screens. Checking my phone, emails, googling. There's still nothing from Ciara, and Ryan has gone suspiciously quiet. I don't know which is worse, her silence or his. I'm running on adrenaline, my appetite as dried up as my eyes.

I googled everything I could find on Mulberry Lodge. Newspaper articles, history of the place, and suspicious deaths. It made for interesting reading. I'm going to hang around until I've joined up a few dots, as there's legwork to do, and it'll take time.

But not today. Today is my birthday.

Ryan downplays birthdays. His own as well as mine. He doesn't like a fuss, and insists I don't waste money on presents. But I spend. What's a girl to do? I try to outdo the surprises every year. If Ryan's jaw drops, I know I've hit the spot. His eyes widen when he rips open the paper on his man tools and gizmos. He's a typical male, the more manuals and attachments the better.

I can see Patrick from the guest room window. He's parked up on the kerb, two wheels on, two wheels off. I wave down, and he flaps for me to hurry up. He's tied a bunch of balloons with coarse green cord to the aerial scut. The pink and red inflatables bobble in excitement.

When I appear, he blushes, spreads out an arm.

'Voila! Thought we'd celebrate in style.'

His fingers desperately try to untangle the bunch of balloons, and I have flashes of clanging cans and newlyweds.

'Wow. They're amazing,' I say. I keep my arms wrapped around my chest against the morning chill. 'Thanks.'

Ryan usually presents me with a small, carefully wrapped box over supper. There's usually something gold, and ridiculously expensive inside. Patrick isn't going for subtle. He flings open the boot, and points at a packed hamper.

'Home-made sandwiches. Home-made quiches, sausage rolls. I've been busy.' He's like a magician with a white rabbit. Two bottles of champagne poke out either end.

'You shouldn't have,' I say, kissing him smack on the lips. He hugs me close, suffocates me with cuddles.

'Why not? Birthdays only happen once a year. Hop in and let's go.'

It feels strange. My first birthday without Ryan since we got married. It's hard, but for Patrick's sake, I need to go with the flow. Enjoy the day. I've never seen him so happy.

I make a brave decision, and to show Patrick what the day means, I turn off my phone.

* * *

Ryan's driving matches his personality. Competitive, fast, and dangerous. He's arrogant, assumes incompetence from other drivers.

Patrick's the complete opposite. His elbow is bent the length of the opened-window seal. Ryan's life, like his car windows, is pretty closed. Artificial ventilation cools his Mercedes, and he's into the latest slick technology.

Patrick rests a couple of fingers on top of the wheel, sliding them back and forth to steer the vehicle. I'm not sure whose driving makes me more nervous. I've never driven with Patrick, but Ryan is a dreadful back-seat passenger. He grips the overhead handle, pummels his feet on imaginary brake pedals, so it's much easier to let him drive.

Ryan plays music up loud, stifling conversation. Opera, classical, concertos, waltzes. Patrick whistles along to Johnny Cash. Patrick's ample hair is spiked up, young dude fashion, although the spikes are collapsing under the weight. Whereas Ryan checks his neat wavy hair in the mirror at traffic lights, Patrick pushes back his flopping fringe as we go along.

We drive northwards, away from Belfast, staying on the coastal route which shadows the shoreline. The view is awesome.

'It's stunning,' I gasp, as the sea pops in and out of view. Shimmering light twinkles on the water. It's like a sheet of frosted glass under the glare of the sun.

'A bit like you.' Patrick turns his head, and smiles. For a moment, things don't seem so bad, and the knots loosen. 'We'll be at the Giant's Causeway in half an hour. Hope you've got your walking shoes on.'

'I remembered.' I look down at my cheap trainers, furious I handed my Nikes to Ciara.

'We'll walk over the basalt columns, build up an appetite. I'll tell you all about the Irish giant Fionn who built the Causeway to reach his enemy, Benandonner in Scotland.'

Patrick turns the music up, and croons to Taylor Swift as his fingers beat rhythm on the wheel, and we let the breathtaking scenery carry on the conversation.

34

FLO

After a couple of hours walking, we settle on a tartan picnic rug, and I throw off my shoes. My feet are on fire. No sooner have I lain out star shape, than Patrick pops a champagne cork, and jumps to one side to catch it.

'My party piece,' he whoops, handing me the cork. He fills two plastic flutes and fizz cascades over the side. 'Happy birthday.' There's little liquid left in either glass when he smashes his against mine.

'Thanks.' I sip slowly and lodge the glass between a couple of rocks on the edge of the rug. Razor spikes poke through and I think of a fakir lying on a bed of nails, but I don't feel a thing. Except a rare moment of contentment.

'The views are amazing,' I say, lounging at an angle. The views from Ramore Head, the watery sun, and the squeal of gulls are hard to beat for atmosphere. It's a little piece of heaven, that's for sure. Patrick needs little work on his sales pitch this time.

Patrick rolls back cling film on the paper plates. 'Help yourself.'

The wind picks up and rips a tear from my eye. Patrick flops down, and starts to chomp on a sausage roll. He tuts as flaky pastry scatters over the rug, but he doesn't care. He seamlessly blends in with the surroundings.

'Have you always lived in Bangor?' I ask.

'No. I just sort of ended up there. It's as nice a place as any.'

His hand inches closer, until our fingers touch.

'I was born in Bantry Bay,' he says. 'Heard of it?'

I inch my fingers away. I've an uneasy feeling. Bantry sounds familiar.

'I've heard of it. Is it north or south?'

I hiccup when the champagne goes down the wrong way.

'South-west Ireland. It is one godforsaken hole. Great for tourists, but bloody awful to grow up in. Nothing but pubs and priests.' Patrick sits up, tucks his knees into his chest.

'I thought you were from Northern Ireland.'

'What? With an accent like mine.' Patrick gives a nervous laugh.

When the sun dips behind a cloud, he pops to the car, and fetches a couple of spare rugs, and tosses one over my head.

'These should keep the draughts out,' he says.

'Ouch.'

When he sits down again, he hands me a small square cardboard box.

'For you.' His face is aglow.

'What is it?'

'Open it.' His hand dips in his pocket, and he produces a lighter.

It's a really small birthday cake, with one candle in the middle. 'FLO' has been iced in pink across the white glaze.

'I made it myself.' Again he's got the kid thing going on. He's so proud that I forget my doubts, and give him a huge hug. 'What's that for? It's only a piece of cake.'

It's much more than a piece of cake. At this moment, I'm ready to let him in. For this moment, anything feels possible. I can work things out with Patrick by my side.

He flicks the lighter, shields the flame behind a palm until he gets purchase on the wick.

'Make a wish,' he says, as I puff out the flame.

I make a list of wishes, no idea of what's about to come.

Only ten minutes later, everything changes. Patrick finally tells me something he thought I ought to know. I didn't believe things could get any worse, as Patrick was the one person in the world I felt I could really trust.

35

FLO

Brother and sister. That's what turned the day into a nightmare. A birthday never to be forgotten. Patrick and Ciara are brother and sister.

The champagne and cake had been oiling our conversation, bringing us close. Closer than we've ever been, until the conversation turned to siblings.

'I'm an only child. I miss having brothers or sisters,' I told him. 'What about you? You never talk about your family.'

Patrick took a few minutes to answer, popping first to the car for the second bottle of champagne. Even as he topped up my flute, I had a strange premonition that he was going to tell me something I didn't want to hear. I kept sipping the bubbles, while he switched to water, confiding he had already three points on his licence and couldn't afford any more.

Even before he spoke, I got a sick feeling in my gut. Why was he taking so long to answer? It was a simple enough question.

'I don't know how to tell you this, but...'

Even through the haze of alcohol, I stiffened. The sun had completely disappeared. I didn't want to hear what he was about to say, but he told me anyway. If I'd been given three guesses, I probably could have worked it out.

'Ciara's my half-sister.'

I couldn't swallow, and had to spit out my drink.

'Go on.'

'It's hard to explain.'

'Try.'

The smiles melted in an instant.

'The Irish suffer from deep-seated guilt. Our mother swore us to secrecy. I was born before my mother finished school, and a few years later she got married. That was when Ciara came along.'

Patrick puffed out the air. Relief at telling me was mingled with fear at my response. He looked as if he was admitting murder, but he was right to be worried. I was beyond furious.

'We don't tell people that we're related. Our mother asked us not to, and even now, we don't stand up to her. Our mother is a bloody nightmare.'

I toyed with smashing the bottle over his head. Why hadn't he told me before? Who would I tell, or who was he scared I might tell?

'You're Ciara's brother?' My question was a spit.

'Half-brother. I should have told you sooner, but so few people know.'

'Yes. You should have. A bit of an understatement.'

I snatched up my bag, tugged at my shoelaces, and staggered off the rug.

'Can we go back? It's bloody freezing.' I tipped my fizz onto the grass and watched the celebrations drain away.

'Sure. I'll tidy up here. You get in the car.'

'Did you know about Ciara's and my plan? That she was going to London to wind Ryan up?'

Patrick shakes out the rug, swinging it all around. Crumbs and pastry flakes scatter like ashes. He doesn't look at me.

'No, I had no idea.' If he wonders what I'm on about, he's too busy packing away the hamper, and worrying about my reaction to what he's told me.

'Listen. I'm sorry I didn't tell you before, but it didn't seem important.'

He has no idea. Or does he?

He came over, steadied his hands on my shoulders, and tried to kiss me. Instead, I turned my face away, and stomped towards the car.

'Let's get back. The weather doesn't look so good.'

With that, we drove back in silence as rain pelted against the windscreen.

36

CIARA

I can't believe Ryan really thinks Flo might come back for her birthday.

I'm at my usual sneaky lookout post in the kitchen, peering out. Ryan couldn't see me, even if he looked, but his head is bent as he ambles up the incline. His mind is miles away.

He's carrying another bunch of flowers. It seems to be a default gift. Birthdays, special occasions, and guilt offerings. At least the ridiculously large bouquet has colour, as he's obviously decided against more thorny red roses.

Flo rolled her eyes when she ran through her birthday routine. Ryan would pop to Blooming Marvellous, the flower shop located between the Tube station and their house. He had an annual ticket on her birthday, Flo joked. She's pretty irritating though, the way she takes it all for granted.

Ryan looks as if he's weighted down. He pauses by the gate, and does a frantic search of his jacket. I can almost hear the sigh of relief when he checks his inside pocket and pats a hand against it. It'll be Flo's present. You've got to be kidding me.

'Every year. A small box. A piece of jewellery.' Flo told me this, how many times?

I anticipated the flowers, and have dug out a motley array of glass vases which once belonged to Ryan's mother. I wonder if he'll recognise them, or prefer to forget.

I've lined them up by the sink. I listen for the key in the lock before I scoot back out into the garden. I arrange myself, photo-shoot model pose, across the sun lounger. I raise a hand to shield my eyes, as I wait for Ryan to appear.

My nails are newly manicured, gratis of the local nail bar. Flo told me where I could find a couple of complimentary passes. I opted for red, and wow, my nails look like talons. At the same time, I topped up the spray tan. My denim shorts and yellow strappy top don't scream *birthday effort*, but Ryan looks as if he could do with a treat.

'Ryan. You're home. You're early.'

He appears by the patio doors, and looks as if he's seen a ghost.

I haven't seen him properly since our pizza lunch up London. I've been playing cat and mouse, but jeez, he looks dreadful. Worse than I imagined, and far worse close up than through the window.

The bouquet seems to wilt in his hand, and falls to the floor.

'Are those for me? They're lovely.' I widen my eyes. Ryan looks as if he's having a minor fit, as he is far too quiet. I sit up, pop my feet on the ground, and bend to pick the flowers up.

'No, they're bloody well not for you.' Ryan makes a swipe for them, and rips the wrapping in the process. Water seeps over his brogues.

'Here. I'll tidy up.'

He stomps back through the kitchen, and chucks the remaining flowers in the bin.

'Are you going to change? I'm cooking supper, so don't be too long.'

When there's no response, I follow him into the hall, and watch him climb the stairs.

'Ryan. I know it's Flo's birthday. I'm sorry she's not here, but we can at least raise a glass.'

Okay, it's a pretty cheap shot, but I want him to know I understand why he's in such a lousy mood.

* * *

Without telling me, Ryan has obviously decided to go for a jog. He was quite a while getting changed, and I didn't hear him move about upstairs, but he suddenly appears, marches past, and slips through the garden gate. He turns right, and starts to jog through the woods.

I hop up, hurry inside and race up the stairs. If I'm not wrong, he'll have been trying to get in touch with Flo, and his laptop should still be in the bedroom.

I should have at least twenty minutes, to see if I can find out if they've been communicating, and what they've been saying.

37

CIARA

There's a crater on the bed where Ryan was sitting. It's still warm, and I snuggle inside.

I'm in luck, because he hasn't turned off his laptop, and it's not asking for a password.

Yep. He's been snitching to Flo all right.

Flo

I need to hear from you. NOW. What the hell is going on? To be honest, I've had enough. I've said I'm sorry, but I'm done. If you don't want to come back, I get it, but can you get this bloody woman out of our house? She can stay in a hotel if she wants a holiday, because I don't want her here.

I hoped you'd come back for your birthday. At least talk things through. If you're not coming back, let me know. I surely deserve that. And by the way,

Happy Birthday. Ryan.

Ryan's angry, that's for sure. I'm not sure whether to be upbeat by his aggressive tone towards Flo, or totally despondent by barbed comments aimed at me. It hurts, no doubt about it.

I get up and wander a few times round the bedroom, then the bathroom, swill mouthwash, and spit it down the plughole. I'm not sure why I'm so shocked by the email. I thought I was getting through, working my magic. Looks as if I'm going to have to up the effort.

Ryan still wants Flo back, but he's nearly at breaking point. As I stare transfixed at my reflection in the bathroom mirror, the ping of a new email sounds on the laptop.

I make a dash out of the bathroom, smashing into the linen basket on the way, and upend a load of Ryan's underpants.

The email from Flo was sent a minute ago.

Ryan
We do need to talk, but not yet. Give me a few more days. Please. You need to let Ciara stay till I get back. It's important. I don't know what she's told you, but you have to trust me on this.
Flo

Not sure who trusts who less. It's a pretty close-run contest.

I feel a bit better, having got both sides of the saga. The lack of XXXs on either email is a positive sign, as far as my plan is concerned.

Suddenly, I freeze. There are the sounds of footsteps down below. Shit. I need to get out of here. I snap shut the laptop, set it back on the pillow at the angle I found it, and sidle along the landing to the spare room.

I close the door in the nick of time, as Ryan is already halfway up the stairs.

38

CIARA

Ryan's mood has definitely lifted since he's been jogging.

He showers, then reappears in the kitchen tousling wet hair, coming at it from both sides, and with a grin on his face. It might not be a grin, but at least it's not a frown, and the scary aggressive look has gone. Flo's email looks as if it's done the trick, telling him she'll be back soon.

He's changed into shorts and a Fred Perry polo, navy and white, as if he's off to play golf.

'Something smells good,' he says sniffing the air.

'Irish stew. What else?' I spear a piece of meat, and hold it out. 'Is it okay?'

'Tastes good,' he says, overdoing the chewing.

It doesn't take him long to register the flowers, the binned ones I've brought back to life.

'I thought they were too nice to chuck,' I tell him.

I don't think he realised how big a bouquet he bought, because the flowers have filled four vases which Flo had hidden at the back of the top cupboard, the one that needs a chair to reach.

'Ryan won't throw out any of his mother's stuff. China. Glasses.

Vases,' Flo told me. 'I've hidden most of it. No idea why he keeps it, but he says it feels wrong to throw out her stuff.'

I wanted to ask Flo why, as he didn't seem to like his mother too much. But I located the Waterford crystal, and got the vases out.

'They look good,' Ryan says.

'We can pretend you bought the flowers for me.' My comment elicits a glimmer of a smile, one that shows a hint of teeth.

He sits down, and pushes one of the tea light candles up the table. At least he doesn't blow it out despite the flickering smoky emissions.

Earlier, he was having such a tantrum that he didn't notice the set table. I found a couple of gaudy wine glasses with gold rims, and *Congratulations* written across the bulb. Ryan lifts one, and swivels it in his hand.

'These were a wedding present,' he says.

'Oh. I didn't realise. Just thought they looked cheerful.' This is not strictly true. They were in a box with a card inside. A wedding present from Adele and Graham.

'Let me serve up. You must be starving.'

Now he's more receptive, I wonder if he notices I've changed clothes. I guessed Flo would dress up for her birthday. Likely something floaty, and feminine. I fingered up and down her party clothes, and back again. The white cotton dress certainly showcases my tan, and I found a cinnamon-smelling cream to moisturise my arms and neck. My hair hangs loose, having binned the scrunchie. It's longer than Flo's, a couple of inches, but tonight I want to look as much like her as possible. It's a special occasion, after all.

The food seems to work its magic. Ryan takes a crust of bread, and wipes clean his plate. He even licks his lips, smacks them together, before he places his knife and fork neatly next to each other.

'I needed that,' he says. 'Thanks.'

'Glad you enjoyed it.'

Everything feels so perfect. A warm summer breeze filters through the patio doors.

'Happy birthday to me!' I announce, holding up my glass. I'm on the tipsy side of drunk.

'What? It's your birthday today as well?'

'Only joking. Definitely not. I'm Gemini all the way, with a scary split personality.'

'You know it's Flo's birthday though?'

'Well, according to her passport, and I didn't really think the flowers were for me.'

39

CIARA

'You don't remember me, do you?' I've now moved on from the tipsy side of drunk, to the daring side of drunk, with a hint of devil-may-care.

'Remember you from where?' He sits up and reels in his legs. His feet look better without the sliders which have been flipped off.

'Ballyholme.'

'Go on. Where in Ballyholme? How would I know you?' He turns awkwardly in his seat. His legs point towards the garden, so he has to twist his neck to look at me. Well, look at me properly, which I think he's been avoiding.

I take my time. This moment has been a long time coming, and I've been patient. He looks anxious, his eyes little slits of concentration. I wonder if he's worked it out.

'Go on,' he repeats.

'Mulberry Lodge.'

'What about Mulberry Lodge?' His Adam's apple bobs up and down as he swallows.

'I used to work there.' I grit my teeth, purse my lips. Prepare for what's about to come.

Ryan pulls up sharply, and knocks his wine glass, the one with *Congratulations* etched in gold, onto the floor. The stem sheers off from the bulb.

'Shit. Shit. Shit.' He stares at the trail of red wine which flows under the table.

I hop up to get a cloth.

'Leave it,' he snaps. 'When?'

'When what?'

'When the fuck were you at Mulberry Lodge?' Ryan's face contorts. It could be the candlelight, but he's getting his angry features back, and a spasm has attacked his jawline.

'Quite a while back.'

'When?' He's now seriously hissing.

'Okay. Okay. When your mother was there.'

'My mother?'

He sounds as if he's going to deny ever having a mother, let alone one in Mulberry Lodge.

'I was there when she died. You might remember me back then as Mary?'

He now looks really scary. Without a word, he's up, tearing off strips of kitchen roll to sop up the mess on the floor. He starts to scrub, back and forth, before he bothers to pick up the fragments of glass.

I'm scared to help in case he slits my throat with a shard. His silence is freaky. I prefer it when he yells. His hands get shakier, and when a splinter sears his palm, blood drips and mingles with the oily mess on the floor.

Part of me wants to put out my hands, help him up, and hold him close. Tell him I'll let it rest, and forget all about Mulberry Lodge. But I can't, as we're in it together.

When he finally sinks back into his seat, the fight seems to drain away. He covers his face with his hands, as if he's waiting for the hangman.

'Don't you remember me? Really?' I ask.

'No. Really, I don't.' He's hard to hear behind his hands.

'Let me jog your memory.'

I empty the rest of the bottle into the remaining wedding-present glass. I'm not sure which bit of the story he's expecting to hear, but I'll only tell him so much.

I wonder how long it will take him to piece the whole thing together.

40

FLO

What's worse? Knowing Ciara is Patrick's sister, albeit half-sister (she could be a twin for all I care), or the fact that Patrick has been lying to me. Okay, by omission, but I'm so goddam angry, it's much the same thing from where I'm standing.

I hop out before Patrick has finished parking.

'See you later?' he asks, so quietly that I guess he's not expecting a reply, let alone to be heard.

I wave over my shoulder, and hover by the guest house entrance. Patrick beeps the horn, a tinny futile fanfare, and I only dare turn once the car has rattled off. Fumes billowing from the exhaust mirror those billowing from my nostrils. Not only have I not spoken a word in the last hour, but I've also been holding my breath. I'm still shaking, and my legs are like jelly.

I look up at my bedroom window which is still open. I could go and lie down, but what then? If there's still no word from Ciara, I'll go even crazier. Not only does my head hurt, but I'm suddenly swamped by sadness. It's my birthday, and I've no one to share it with.

I look left, then right. Left leads to the desolation of the beach, and right leads into town. I check my phone, miserable that I'm back on a ten-minute vigil, but there's still no messages. Nothing.

At the moment, I'm furious with Ciara, and Patrick, and for once, less so with Ryan. Ryan owned up to what he did with Olivia at least, and until I see him, I'll not get answers to the murder. He's got a get-out-jail card if he can convince me why he did it. If it's the right answer, I might be able to forgive him. If it's the wrong one? Who knows, because I'm not there yet.

It's still only six, so I decide to turn right and stroll up the High Street. I glance vacantly into shop windows, and mosey past the estate agents' I visited a couple of days ago. The *Closed* sign is turned outwards, and through the glass, there's no sign of Rowan.

The crossroads at the top mirror my indecision. As it's still early, I decide to carry straight on. Lack of people anywhere makes me feel even lonelier. The streets are all deserted, and everywhere is strangely quiet, despite the fact it's not raining.

When I reach the roundabout, there's a sudden buzz of activity. With each step, the noise gets louder, until it's deafening. It sounds as if a live band has started up, and an open door on the corner of Argyle Street tells me where the din is coming from. Empty metal tables and chairs are scattered on the pavement outside O'Malley's pub, the name of which is painted in green and gold letters across a rotting fascia board.

Why not? It's my birthday, and getting drunk seems as good a plan as any.

41

FLO

O'Malley's is like a Wild West saloon. Irish music blasts round the place, and no one bats an eyelid when I wander in.

The earlier champagne is still in my system, so I'm not too worried about appearances. My hair's windswept, like on a bad hair day, and I'm certainly not dressed for The Ritz. A quick glance at other customers, and I fit right in. The cheap trainers could even be a bit fancy, and as for being a woman on her own, no one is looking my way. A high-backed stool at the end of the bar has my name on it.

Before I've even sat down, a barman with a shiny bulbous nose, and gaps in his teeth, is in front of me.

'Evening. What can I get you, love?'

He wets the words with a swig from a pint glass, and rubs down the counter with a sodden cloth before chucking a couple of beer mats my way.

I unravel my woolly scarf, and look over his shoulder. Champagne by the glass is unlikely.

'A glass of white wine?'

'Coming up. I'm Jimmy by the way.' His broad smile, easy manner, reminds me of Ciara. It's the Irish thing again.

'Hi,' I say. I'm not a fan of giving my name to strangers at the best of times, but Jimmy has already got his back to me, filling a glass to the brim from an already opened bottle. No skimpy measures here. From the way he's pouring, it looks like small, medium and large measures are the same.

Jimmy isn't a looker, and even the dim lighting doesn't disguise his weathered appearance. The whites of his eyes are yellow, and match the few teeth he seems to have left. But he sure likes to talk.

'You on holiday?' His large, calloused hands settle on the counter, and a chesty cough gets tagged on to the question.

'Yes. You could say that.' I smile, and knock back half the glass.

Jimmy excuses himself when a customer sidles up to the bar, but winks and tells me not to go anywhere.

'I'll be back.' He grins through a couple of teeth.

It's been at least fifteen minutes since I checked my phone. I'm like an alcoholic who has lasted an extra five minutes before giving in. Despite the noise, the gulps of wine, my heart ratchets up when I see I've got a new email from Ryan.

While I decide whether to look or not, a WhatsApp message pings through from Patrick. I now do the bravest thing I've done in a while, and mute my phone and slip it in my bag.

Jimmy soon returns. He must have thrown the drink at the customer, he's been that quick.

I'm in two minds as to whether to make tracks, but the wine is comforting, the darkness and noise distracting. And the draughty bedroom at the guest house is about attractive as a room in the Bates Motel.

Jimmy makes up my mind for me, and refills my glass without asking.

'On the house,' he says.

It's too late to refuse, but my glass is so full there's no space at the top of it, and I have to lean over and lap like a cat. It sends Jimmy into convulsions, but he's not judging, just enjoying himself.

'So, you're on holiday. Over from the mainland, if I'm not mistaken?'

I nod, struggling with a surfeit of liquid in my mouth.

'You remind me of someone. Hmm.' He does that thinking thing, looks up at the ceiling, curls his tongue against his upper lip.

How do I know what he's about to say? Am I that drunk? Okay, Rowan let slip that Mary McCluskey/Ciara McCluskey liked to drink, but I can't remember if he mentioned O'Malley's. He might have done, but I'm too far gone to care.

'Anyone special?' I yell at Jimmy over the noise. When he turns his ear towards me, and still can't hear, he gives in and turns the music down.

'Thank God for that. I can now hear myself think. Anyone special?' He mulls it over. 'Oh, just someone who used to drink here. You're a dead ringer.'

My shoulders stiffen. I swivel my birthday drink, round and round on the sticky surface.

'Mary McCluskey. A right wild one she was,' he adds.

Leaving now is the last thing on my mind.

42

FLO

'You're the second person in Bangor who's told me I look like this Mary. Hoping it's a compliment.'

I'm keen to listen, but starting to freak by being told by several people now that I look like Ciara. Patrick, Rowan and now Jimmy. It was the first thing Patrick said when he saw us together.

'She's not from around here. Mary's from the south, came up from Bantry looking for work.' As Jimmy talks, little slivers of skin, like flakes of peeling paint, drizzle over his shirt, and his face is as weathered as the fascia board out front.

'Does she still come in here?' My throat rasps from shouting. Even with the music turned down, the noise is deafening.

'Yes. She still comes by. She changed her name to Ciara, God knows why. Ideas above herself, that's for sure.'

Wine gurgles back up my throat, makes me hiccup. Jimmy waits till I catch my breath.

'I met her,' I say. 'She's got a brother who works near where I'm staying.'

'Brother? No, that's not her then. She's an only child. Never mentioned any brothers or sisters, and she's been here often enough. Also occasionally helps out behind the bar.'

Jimmy excuses himself, and is about to serve another customer, when he adds, 'She's friends with Patrick who runs the pub in Ballyholme. But they're not related.'

With Jimmy at the far end of the bar, I dig out my phone. Again. Not sure what I'm expecting. There's still only the one unopened email from Ryan, but Patrick has left three new messages in the last ten minutes. He's apologised in six different sentences. Rows of sad emojis are hard to ignore.

Mellowed from what Jimmy's just told me, I message back.

No worries. Thanks for a lovely picnic and for telling me about you and Ciara. X

No sooner have I pressed send, than a new line of emojis appear. A long line of red hearts, and clinking champagne classes. Finally, a GIF of a birthday cake with one candle in the middle flashes up. I try to hold back the tears, but they still slide down my cheeks.

Opening Ryan's email isn't as easy. It's pretty threatening, his tone far removed from Patrick's. I need to calm him down, stop him doing anything rash, as I don't want him going to prison, and certainly not because of Ciara. I reply, again, that he needs to let Ciara stay, leaving out kisses, and mention of my birthday.

I drink up, wave at Jimmy and head for the exit. Jimmy waddles quickly for someone with such a beer belly, and we reach the door at the same time. He holds it wide, and says he hopes to see me soon.

On the street, I zip up my raincoat, and look down at my cheap trainers. Rain sploshes over them, and soaks through the pink fabric, the water puddling round my socks. They'll be the first thing to bin when I get back. I'll fly home at the weekend, but first I've a couple of people to visit.

When I get back to London, I'll find out why Ryan killed his mother. Did she plead with him to end her misery? Or did he kill her to end his? I'll look in the whites of his eyes.

Only then, will I know what to do.

43

CIARA (MARY)

Seven Years Previously

Mulberry Lodge was where it all started, and Mr Harrison junior had set the ball rolling.

Mulberry Lodge was the most depressing place to work. The smell of death hung in the air like a toothless dog's blanket. Thick and rancid. Sunlight screamed taunts through the bolted windows, while decaying residents jiggled their legs back and forth, and let out the most bloodcurdling screams.

It was a Friday. I remember the day, and the date. It was Friday the thirteenth. Lucky for some, unlucky for others. Especially unlucky for Mr Harrison senior.

Around 8 a.m., the front door swung open, letting in a whoosh of wintry air. Mr Harrison's son, Bill, sauntered up towards reception. He plonked his pale hands on the counter, and snapped scruffy brown brogues to attention.

'Morning, Mary. How's life with you today?'

'Good morning, Mr Harrison. I'm grand, thank you.' I glanced at the clock. 'You're earlier than usual.'

'Got a busy day ahead. Thought I'd pop in and see the old git before breakfast.' He had the laugh of a dirty old man.

Balding, with a line of ginger hairs running left to right across his forehead, Bill Harrison was the sort of person you'd never remember. His chalk-white complexion was dappled with liver spots which looked like an encroaching disease. And his voice had the drone of a dentist's drill.

But I was interested in Mr Harrison, and what an old devil he was. I'd been watching him for months. And listening. Before I bought the video recorder, courtesy of eBay, I'd eavesdrop outside Mr Harrison senior's room when Bill visited.

On Friday the thirteenth, I made sure Mr Harrison junior signed the register.

He extracted a leaky biro from his pocket, and tried to scribble his illegible scrawl in the visitor's book. I had to hand him another pen.

'Here. Try this one, Mr Harrison. Shall I throw yours away before it ruins your jacket?'

'Thank you, Mary.'

He handed over the leaky pen, and tried again to sign the book. His signature was no more than a wiggly line with a couple of peaks and a couple of troughs. But it would do the trick. It was all the evidence I needed to prove that he had been at Mulberry Lodge on Friday the thirteenth.

'You go on through. Your dad's had his breakfast, and should be wide awake.'

My eyes followed him down the corridor. He was stooped, walked with a rhythmic limp, and had more than once been mistaken for one of the patients.

Once he was out of sight, I bent down, switched on the video player. It was pretty fuzzy, but I stared at the screen. Bill Harrison soon came into view. He locked the door, checked it a couple of times, before facing his father, and shaking his skeletal hand.

Then he proceeded to kill his father, smother him with a pillow. I clapped my hands together.

I had guessed right.

44

CIARA

Six Years Previously

It was a year later that Ryan murdered his mother.

When he banged into me some four hours after signing the visitors' book with his own gold-tipped Parker pen, he failed to recognise me. He had no idea I was the receptionist from Mulberry Lodge.

The buzz, after the suspicious death of Mr Harrison senior at the Lodge, quickly died away. Apathy over old people's deaths, especially in a home full of dementia patients, meant Bill Harrison got away with murder. Well, that's what he thought.

About six months later, I began to suspect Ryan Bartlam might be having the same idea as Bill Harrison. Ryan definitely didn't get on too well with his mother. I have loads of video recordings taken before the 16 June. Even without sound, it was pretty clear that Ryan and his mother argued. He stomped round the room, glowered at her, and once even poured a cup of hot tea over her. He told me she'd spilled it, as she was getting very shaky.

The sixteenth of June was the day things changed forever. That was when Ryan Bartlam killed his mother. Like Bill Harrison, he took a pillow, clamped it over her face, and smothered her.

I'm definitely a Gemini. Born 15 June. Split personality. Sweet or bitchy, depending on mood. Caring and conniving in equal measure. My worst side often pairs with hangovers, and morning-after regrets. Patrick blames everything on the alcohol, and calls me a tart.

'You're screwed up. Forget the split personality crap,' he says. 'It wouldn't matter when you were born. You're just crazy.'

Okay, I'm an Irish drinker. Beats the teetotal bigots by a long chalk. The sixteenth was a Tuesday. I clocked off early from work. It had been quite a day, and I was still in shock.

I also needed a few hair-of-the-dog shots after my birthday, so after getting showered and changed, I settled in a corner of O'Malley's pub at the top of the High Street. That was when Ryan Bartlam walked in. Back then, he called himself Ryan Carter. A calculated pseudonym, I realised later.

Women are a rare sight in O'Malley's. Like virgins in a brothel, but in my short skirt, low-cut top, I was up for some fun. I was already three sheets to the wind when the hunky Englishman walked in. He was *my type of man*, that's for sure.

I was buzzing, and throwing money and caution to the wind.

'Jimmy. A top-up, please. And one for yourself.' I threw a £20 note across the counter, and told the barman to keep the change.

'I thought it was your birthday yesterday,' Jimmy said, with a tut, and a roll of his eyes. 'What are you celebrating today?'

Wouldn't he like to know? Instead, I told him I was planning a birthday year.

'Do you know what a birthday year is?' Jimmy shook his head.

'I'm going to keep the celebrations going for the full twelve months. Why cram all the fun into one day? Cheers,' I screeched over the music.

Jimmy ignored me, and went to serve Ryan, who was standing so close, I could smell the earthy, woody smell of aftershave. The smell was so strong, as if he was trying to drown out the stench of death.

He was already smashed, but knocked back two neat whiskeys, one after the other. He swivelled the stool beside mine, and collapsed into it. After a third measure, he asked for ice to water down the whiskey.

'Ice,' I yelled. 'You've got to be kidding me. The Irish *do-not-dilute-their-drink*.'

He smiled at me. Jeez, he was bloody gorgeous. The type of man I spent all my spare time dreaming about. Chocolate brown eyes, full lips, and a lopsided grin that couldn't get any sexier.

'What can I get you? Same again?' he asked. When he looked my way, I felt weak.

'Go on then.' I wiggled my empty glass, but Jimmy was slow to move. 'I'm Mary, by the way.' Ryan took my hand and kissed it.

'Ryan. Ryan Carter. Is this your local?' he asked.

'Yep. Sad, isn't it?'

I wondered, in the weeks, months, and years that followed, if Ryan hadn't recognised me from Mulberry Lodge because he'd been so drunk. Or was it because I looked so different in my tarty gear, than I did in blue nylon overall and starched white cap. The mandatory caps were so neat fitting, that I could have been bald underneath, for all anyone knew.

Ryan was charming. He wasn't like Patrick, critical, and disapproving. We chatted, made small talk, and he told me he worked in banking. Some large institution in London. He said he was visiting friends in Bangor, no mention of a mother. He asked me what I did for a living.

Since he didn't recognise me, I didn't tell him. Working in an old people's home isn't that sexy, and I was already falling madly in love.

Also, I didn't think he'd be too keen to hang around if he knew I'd been working at Mulberry Lodge all day. Especially as it had only been four hours since he'd murdered his mother.

45

CIARA

The morning after I met Ryan in O'Malley's, my head was more than fuzzy. It throbbed, and the pain felt as if someone had clobbered it with a mallet.

It took a while to remember what had happened, and it became the first day of a very long wait. I recalled being pissed off that Ryan hadn't recognised me from the nursing home. Then I remembered not caring at all. He told me, more than once, that I was beautiful, and then screwed me in the back of his hire car. It took half an hour of staggering, and giggling, before we found the Fiat Panda parked half a mile up the coast road.

On the way home, I tore off my heels, and ripped my bare feet to shreds as I hobbled along the beach. I sang 'Beach Baby Beach' at the top of my voice.

I gave Ryan my number, and he swore on his mother's life (ha, ha... perhaps that's when I should have owned up) that he'd call. He was going to be around for a few more days, and I was so excited. He fancied a tour of the Titanic Centre, or a trip round the Antrim coast, take in the Giant's Causeway. He was happy to drive.

The waiting was excruciating. Excitement and anticipation

soon turned to despair. I stared at my mobile for days, willing the suave, drop-dead gorgeous Englishman to call, and whisk me away.

But Ryan didn't call. He simply disappeared. I wasn't overly worried at first, confident that I could track him down. I had his name, and the name of the bank where he worked. It couldn't be that difficult. There was also a next-of-kin contact number at the home, but by the time I gave in and tried the number, it was disconnected.

The first few days after he disappeared, I clung to hope. Men do lose women's phone numbers, and there might be a wife or girlfriend in the background. There could have been a number of reasons why he didn't phone. Who was I kidding? I knew I was grasping at straws.

The police sniffed around after his mother's death, but eventually put it down to natural causes, the same way they did with Mr Harrison. I don't even know if the police spoke to Ryan in person, but they refused to give me his details. Mulberry Lodge, its reputation tarnished by two suspicious deaths, was quite happy to sign off on the death certificates to keep the snoops away.

If Ryan had phoned me, made some excuse as to why he couldn't see me again, I mightn't have been so contrived. Determined in my plans.

He was impossible to track down, having covered all angles. I'd been a sordid one-night stand, and had virtually given up the hunt, when Flo Bartlam appeared on the scene. And bingo...

I've got my chance, and now I'm after much more than money.

46

CIARA

The Present Day

Ryan still has absolutely no idea who I am. There's not the faintest flicker of recognition.

He doesn't remember me as Mary dressed in blue nylon overalls and white starched cap, but it kind of sucks that he hasn't twigged I was the woman he picked up in O'Malley's. Shortly after killing his mother.

'Why don't we go into the lounge, and I'll remind you who I am.'

Ryan looks blank. Not sure if he's delirious from drink or shock at hearing that I worked at Mulberry Lodge. Either way, he nods, and sits a moment. I can feel his eyes on my back, as I wiggle my hips, and flounce off towards the lounge.

I fall into the plush cream leather sofa, and stretch my legs along its length. Ryan wanders in, gripping a new wine glass like a security blanket. Plonked in a matching recliner, he stares at me.

Hard to tell if he's trying to unnerve me, or trying to remember my face. Lines of concentration have settled across his forehead, round his mouth, and even on a cheek.

Flo warned me that Ryan is controlling, and when he's not sure what's going on, he asks question, after question.

'If I go for a drink with the girls, it'll be: *Where did you go? Who else was there? What did you talk about?* He's not really interested in the answers, but hates secrets. Total control makes him tick.'

I'm preparing myself for an interrogation. At least I've been warned, although he's slow to kick off.

'Go on then. Remind me. How should I remember you?'

'You used to come and visit your mum. I was working at Mulberry Lodge at the time. You must remember Mulberry Lodge, surely.' It's tempting to bait, but I need to rein in the hook. One bite at a time. 'I met you there quite a few times.'

'Why don't I remember you then?' His hair gets a serious tousle, his fingers raking through from all angles.

'Probably the uniform. I doubt surgical outfits are your thing.' He doesn't smile, but keeping it light certainly helps my nerves.

'Did we ever talk? About anything other than my mother?'

'No. Not really. You were always in a rush.' I take a huge breath, stuff a cushion under my coccyx. 'I don't think you were too fond of your mother. You called her "a cantankerous old bitch".'

He doesn't question how I remember his words, but is quick to agree.

'You've hit the nail on the head there.'

He takes out a ruffled hankie, wipes the base of his glass, and sets it down. He's had enough of this particular line of conversation.

'That's why you seem familiar. Sorry. I'd really no idea.' His wrinkles dissipate, one at a time. He really thinks that's all there is to it, as far as our acquaintance goes.

He looks relieved if a tad smug. He still believes, even though I'm sitting here, that he's got away with it. Well, got away with sin number one: killing his mother. I wonder how long it'll take for him to twig that I'm involved in a second sin he committed shortly afterwards.

All in good time. If Ryan has heard enough, that suits me fine. Now, I've work to do.

Let's see how easily he'll be tempted tonight.

47

CIARA

It doesn't take Ryan long to loosen up, and talk about other things. Eyes wide, I paint on my rapt expression. Patrick says I should be an actress.

Jeez, it certainly does the trick. Ryan doesn't half love the sound of his own voice. Once he gets going, he doesn't stop. He loves fast cars, *Top Gear* his favourite programme. Rambling, hiking, marathons, swimming, cycling, and all things outdoorsy. My engrossed expression is working too well.

He throws out a token question about my hobbies, but he's not really interested, impatient to restart on his own. Wine, chat, and the locked-in heat, soon knock aside Ryan's stiff-upper-lip aloofness. He's definitely got good old Irish roots. We're a match made in heaven.

While he talks, I slide off the sofa, and gently pull down the white cotton dress. It's currently riding up over my thighs. There's a hiccup in Ryan's flow, as I rub both hands down the soft fabric.

The curtains on the window at the end of the lounge that faces the street are drawn. But the ones on the window facing the back garden are wide open. Earlier, I turned on a flimsy set of fairy lights that runs along the top of a ridiculously high fence that separates us from the neighbours.

It's pretty spooky outside, but the smoky glow is rather romantic. I must be drunk, because the shadows weaving across the weird, triangular-shaped patch of grass are more on the macabre side of romantic. They're like black ghosts, constantly on the move.

'Top up?' I peer through the green bottle, give it a shake, but it's empty.

'Sorry. I polished it off,' Ryan says.

'No worries. I opened a second bottle earlier. I'll go and get it.'

He doesn't object, and even offers the hint of a smile. The fight is definitely draining from him. He looks beat, quite unaware that I'm homing in for the knock-out punch.

As I pass the hall mirror, I push my hands either side of my breasts, wiggle, and nudge them upwards to show a hint of cleavage. At least I chose one dress of Flo's that doesn't button round the neck.

I get the new bottle from the fridge, and when I get back, Ryan looks to be dozing off.

'Voila!'

Her jerks back to the present. I take my time refilling his glass. Think snails, and I stick my chest plonk in his eyeline as I bend over.

'Thanks,' he says.

'My pleasure.' I aim for film star husky. I don't sit down, but hover. I'm nearly as good at hovering as I am at listening.

A couple of seconds. That's all it takes for Ryan to stretch out an arm, and take my hand.

He pulls his legs together, and hauls me roughly on top of him. He prises my thighs apart until I'm straddling him. His hands push inside my now-gaping dress, and release a bare breast. I gasp, as he teases the nipple.

Ryan's breathing speeds up, and I ruck the dress up, willing him on. Beneath me I feel his hard arousal. We both need this. Well, I certainly do.

As he thrusts inside me, I rear back, and close my eyes. It's been a long wait, but this will be more than a one-night stand.

Ryan Bartlam will not forget me again.

48

FLO

After my night in O'Malley's, my birthday hangover is so bad, that Ciara, Ryan, and Patrick aren't my first concerns.

Four cups of coffee, a couple of paracetamol tablets, and it all comes flooding back. My stomach growls, although the last thing I want is food. But I'm so dizzy, I need to eat.

I grab a couple of pieces of toast from the breakfast buffet, and wash them down with more coffee. By the time I leave the guest house, I'm seriously shaking.

The cold air soon knocks aside the sleep. I stride up through Bangor, pick my way through a maze of side streets, until I get to my destination. The narrow street consists of a small row of red-brick terrace houses. If I was intrigued by the street's name – Rotten Row – the reality is worse than I imagined. The place is deserted apart from a couple of kids practising hire-wire acrobatics along a narrow brick wall.

Rowan from the estate agents' let slip where Mr Connor, the owner of Mulberry Lodge lived. Rowan wasn't sure of the house number, but was certain it was on the end of the row. He didn't ask why I wanted to know, just seemed happy to be of help.

Number ten is the house on the end. A rusting 'Beware of the Dog' sign is nailed to the gate, and, as if on cue, a ferocious growl drools through the letter box. A couple of steps and I'm at the front door, and the barking ratchets up, as the dog throws itself against the door.

'Shut up, Buster. For God's sake, give me a break.' The bark turns to a whimper as a key rattles in the lock. The door cracks open, and a pair of eyes appear in the slit.

'Yes?' Half-closed, puffy eyes squint at me.

'Mr Connor?' I ask

'Who's asking?'

'My name's Flo Bartlam. Could I ask you about Mulberry Lodge?'

'As long as you're not police, or it's not money you're after.'

My smile seems to do the trick, because Mr Connor closes the door, undoes the chain, and hauling at the dog's collar, invites me in.

'Excuse the mess,' he says. Bit of an understatement. I sidestep over piles of brown envelopes strewn across the hall. Damp dog breath mingles with a stench of fried food, and I swallow hard against the nausea.

On the plus side, Buster is a wiry mongrel, not a Rottweiler. It dips back and forth, wagging its tail, with a salivating tongue the shape of a shoehorn. *Bark worse than its bite* seems to be its thing.

'In here. What did you say your name was again?' Mr Connor smiles, all wobbly double chins, and points to an armchair.

'Flo Bartlam. I believe you were, still are, the owner of Mulberry Lodge. I wonder if you remember a girl who worked there, Mary McCluskey?'

He falters before slumping into a chair and pushing his bony feet into a pair of tatty tartan slippers.

'I remember Mary. How could I forget? A right wild one. What is you want to know?'

To be honest, I'm not sure what I want to know but maybe if I listen to a rambling tongue, I'll get some answers. Piece together more of the jigsaw.

'Mary worked with us for a few years. She was popular, hardworking. The patients seemed to like her.' Mr Connor catches his breath, and I can hear the chest rattle from where I'm sitting. 'Except for a Mr Harrison. After his father died, he had it in for the home. And for Mary especially.'

'Why? What had she done?'

'He maintained negligence had been the reason for his father's death. But he didn't keep it up for long.'

Buster whimpers as Mr Connor's chest wheezes from the effort of talking.

'Oh. Any reason?'

'Poor bugger hanged himself. Absolutely no idea why, but by then the nursing home had a tarnished reputation.'

Buster bounds onto his master's lap, slaps a wet tongue across his cheeks.

'Was that when the home closed down?'

'No. It closed a while after. Another patient died, again under suspicious circumstances. Can't remember the name now, but the press were all over it. To be honest, by then I'd had enough, and decided to shut up shop. Now I'm trying to sell the bloody place.'

'Was it a woman patient who died? A Mrs Bartlam, by any chance?'

Buster has begun a low growl, and is baring two rows of tiny, ragged teeth. Mr Connor's calloused hands have trouble holding him down.

'Yes. I think that was her name. Why? Did you know her?'

'Yes. She was my mother-in-law.'

* * *

Half an hour later, I take a detour back via Groomsport, a quaint fishing village a couple of miles round the coast. I gulp in the fresh, salty sea air. Questions swirl round in my head.

Why did Mr Harrison junior kill himself? What was suspicious about the death of Ryan's mother? Had these suspicions been reported? What was the link between Mary and the two deaths? If any.

If Mr Harrison junior killed himself, perhaps Mary/Ciara had started to blackmail him with photos and videos similar to those she sent me.

I sit on a bench facing out to sea. I pull a beanie from my pocket, yank it down over my ears, and stare into the distance. If my hunch is right, Ciara has been planning to blackmail Ryan all along. Maybe he left Ireland before she got the chance.

Now she's got her chance. She's found Ryan, and with all the evidence, she's surely only got one thing on her mind. Blackmail.

I suddenly realise that I haven't checked my phone all morning. What with the hangover, and the visit to Mr Connor, I forgot to even look. Before I get up, I turn my phone on. My jaw tightens when I see a couple of new messages from Ryan.

When are you coming back? Please let me know. Missing you more than ever. XXXX

He sent the first message at 2 a.m. I key in a reply before reading the second one which was sent shortly after at 3 a.m.

Soon. Not sure when exactly. But it won't be long.

Maybe it's the time of the messages that makes me uneasy: I know Ryan. After he read the email I sent him last night, he would

have been relieved to hear I was coming back soon, and that
should have sent him into his usual heavy slumber. Also the
wording is telling me something. I reread his second message
several times.

We really need to talk. Things are so complicated. I want to sort things
out, show you how much I care. Please come home soon. XXXXXXXX

Also, why so many kisses? He's either drunk, or else... OMG. It
reads like a guilt text. What the hell is going on?

49

CIARA

The recording is short, fuzzy, but our voices are unmistakable.

Ryan talks dirty when making love, and 'Come here, you slut,' is at odds with the plummy accent. His words slur, but they're clear enough. If Flo is still dithering about whether to give Ryan another chance, last night's reel should make up her mind. I know I shouldn't have taken it, but just in case.

I set off early for my interview at the Winterton Arms pub. The advert in the free newspaper caught my eye, as there was accommodation to go with the job, a bedsit above the bar. I need to be ready for when Flo gets back, as she'll no doubt be quick to throw me out. The bedsit will be temporary, until Ryan and I find somewhere more permanent. I will get my well-deserved happy-ever-after with the man of my dreams. For now, needs must.

The landlord, red faced and agitated, waves at me as I enter his pub. He is wiping down the counter from the customers' side with a dirty rag. His maroon-coloured thickset neck, and ruddy hardened complexion tell me he likes a drink or two with the punters.

'Mr Burrell?'

'Hi. You must be Ciara,' he says, pronouncing it 'Carrie'. I don't correct him, as he's puffing heavily, too breathless to engage. 'Have a seat.' He nods at a bar stool, and squeezes through a narrow gap to get behind the bar.

'Nice place you've got,' I lie. Googling threw up images of an olde-worlde pub, oak beams, and plush velvet. A stench of stale beer and damp dishcloths are what's really going on.

'Thanks. It's okay.' His eyes shine, as they look round the room. 'Right, Carrie. Have you had much bar experience?'

Burrell whistles through thick grey whiskers, meaty fingers twisting the hairs.

'Drink?' he asks, picking up a glass, scooting it up and down a couple of times under an optic, and throwing the contents down his own throat. His eyes water, but he refills the glass before repeating his question.

'No thanks. Yes, I've got plenty of bar experience. I've recently moved to London and keen to find work.' I nestle my chest on top of the bar.

'I'll take your word for it.' A hoarse laugh wheezes up from his chest as he slaps his hands together. 'What say I give you a trial for a week or two. How does that sound?'

'Sounds good to me.'

'When can you start?'

'Monday any good?'

He spits on a palm, extends a pack of sausage fingers, and says, 'Put it there.'

Before I can object, my hand is in a soggy vice-like grip.

'We can do the paperwork then. Would you prefer a coffee? Hope you're not a teetotaller.' He laughs, and smacks his hands together again.

As Burrell goes off to make coffee, I mosey over to a seat by an opened back door, and breathe in the freshness.

Outside, rickety furniture covered in green algae is dotted around. Beer glasses, as green as the algae, have mould inside. A pile of unopened red umbrellas are stacked against a fence. The miserable image mocks my relief at being offered a job, but it stokes my determination.

On impulse, I snap a picture of the garden, and attach it to a message.

Hi Flo. Recognise where I am?

I watch the screen, and within seconds, Flo is typing. I'm a bit surprised, as her messages have virtually dried up, but I can gauge her mood by the speed of her response.

Burrell waddles over with a huge mug of milky liquid. As he plonks it on the table, milk slops over a couple of biscuits on the saucer.

'Welcome aboard.' His smile bares a few yellow decaying teeth, and I think of Jimmy from O'Malley's. They're more than a little alike.

I look down at my screen.

Where the hell are you? It's been a week and not a bloody word. What the f is going on?

I sip the tepid coffee, bitter as hell, and add a couple of sugar lumps. With the spoon, I shovel up the wet biscuit mixture and suck it off.

Four new messages appear, one after another, as if a virus has crippled the network. By the time I finish the coffee, Flo has sent a total of six messages.

Don't sweat. I'm having a great time. Ryan is fine. Enjoy Patrick and catch up soon.

After I've sent the short reply, I turn the phone off.

On my way out, a couple of customers trickle by, and I check my watch.

Time's ticking. Tick tock. Tick tock.

50

FLO

Ciara's message comes as a shock. I'd almost given up hearing from her, and have been preparing for a face-to-face showdown back in London.

My white knuckles grip the steaming mug of tea. The Harbour Café is like a sauna, but I'm shivering like crazy. I've got so many layers on, that perspiration is making me colder. I unwind my scarf which feels as if it's choking me.

I'm on my third mug of tea. The pink-aproned teenager behind the counter has tried unsuccessfully to tempt me with sausage rolls and freshly baked scones. I think she can tell by looking at me, that I'm not in a good place.

I can't face going back to the hotel, and since I left Mr Connor's, I've taken ownership of the table by the window. A vain hope was that the view of the marina might calm me down. The boats bob up and down. Barren masts without mainsails dance like a chorus line of dancers every time a sudden gust of wind shocks the boats to life.

The early sun has already gone, and it's not even lunchtime. A customer barges in, letting in a gasp of cold air, and shakes out a sodden umbrella.

'Bloody awful weather,' she says, rolling her eyes at me, yet managing a smile.

The first time I visited Ballyholme with Ryan, we were so in love. Together forever. That's what I believed. Ballyholme seemed so magical, but when you're in love even the Arctic Circle would have its attractions.

I reply to Ciara's message instantly, and check out the picture she attached. It's of the pub garden of the Winterton Arms which is a mile from our house. Ryan and I dropped by once, but never again. We'd been cycling, desperate for a cold lager, and popped in. I remember Ryan couldn't get out fast enough. A *dirty old man's pub* he called it.

I'm scared by my level of fury. If Ciara was nearby, I don't know what I'd do. Probably kill her the way I feel.

I fire off message after message when I know she's online. When I get her terse reply, I feel even worse. She's toying with me, deliberately trying to make me suffer. But why? Why doesn't she just make her move, and start pressing for money? Or go to the police.

I now know how it feels when your *blood boils*. I seriously need to calm down. I lash a hand hard against the tabletop, and my phone flies off. A couple of old ladies turn, do a bit of whispering, and look away.

What the hell does Ciara want?

I've sort of lost track of why I'm protecting Ryan, and why I feel protective towards him.

The shock of the videos of him smothering his mother should have been the icing on the blame cake, the final nail that sent me to the divorce lawyer. But I know the damage his mother did to him. It doesn't justify murder, but what if it was a mercy killing? He told me often enough how his mother guilt-tripped him, promising to down a whole bottle of paracetamol with her whiskey, and that she'd had enough. What if this is why he did it.

I try to remember back. Ryan wasn't particularly sad when his mother died, so I never took much note. If anything, he seemed relieved, glad she was gone. 'Died peacefully in her sleep,' he told me. Did he cry? I can't remember any tears.

Surely I'd have known if he'd planned to kill her? If it had been planned in advance, would he have acted any differently?

I can't forget that he mentioned, in passing, more than once, how the nursing home was eating into his mother's savings. If the police did question him, even after all this time, wouldn't protecting his legacy be motive enough for murder?

'By the time she finally does kick the bucket, there'll be nothing left,' he'd said.

Recall makes me stiffen. Pins and needles shoot up my arms, and my heart won't calm down. The fact that Ciara has taken control of Ryan's and my life is skewing my perspective. I can't calm down.

I finally give in and take out the glossy brochure that has been languishing at the bottom of my bag for a few days. I lay it on the Formica-topped table and use my palms to flatten it out. The shiny content, with pages and pages of bright blue and yellow blurb, is doing a sales pitch. Rugged landscapes, patchwork fields, country lanes with rough stone walls, and even the cemeteries suddenly seem appealing. That's how bad a state I'm in. I read the blurb, which ties in with Patrick's spiel.

Patrick can be very persuasive. Hanging around in no-man's land isn't doing me any favours, and I'm not quite ready to go back. Perhaps he's right, and I should see a bit of Ireland while I'm here. And if I go with him to Bantry Bay, I can see for myself where he and Ciara grew up.

Bantry is the perfect haven in West Cork for outdoor activities. Whether you like to immerse yourself in nature and walk the hills of our beautiful landscapes or enjoy Bantry Bay through sailing, boat trips, our islands or fishing, it's all here for you. Pony-trekking, golf, stunning gardens, and so many more outdoor activities are waiting for you in Bantry.

As I relax into the descriptions, losing myself in snippets about the Irish Rebellion, I have a eureka moment. Bantry is somewhere I need to go. Maybe I've been looking in the wrong places for answers.

Although Ryan's mother is dead, Patrick and Ciara's mother is very much alive. She suddenly seems like a vital piece of a jigsaw. Something about Patrick's and Ciara's background all at once seems important.

'You can meet my mother, but heaven help you. From what you've told me, she's not unlike Ryan's mother.' I remember Patrick's words. They're ringing in my ear.

I lift my phone, and text Patrick.

Okay. I'll come to Bantry with you. See you in the morning. xx

Patrick comes straight back with a thumbs up and a long row of kisses.

Then I text Ryan.

Ryan, I'll be back next week. Don't tell Ciara. I'll explain everything when I see you.

I leave out the kisses and turn my phone off. I then start scribbling on a serviette a rough shopping list. Rucksack. Cagoule. Walking shoes.

As I head out into the thick persistent sheet of rain, I smile. Patrick tells me that rain in Ireland is wetter than anywhere else in the world. He's certainly not wrong.

I turn my face upwards, hoping the downpour will wash away the fear and anger.

The way I'm feeling, I could be standing here a long time.

51

CIARA

Flo had told me all about the Hardens' garden party. Freddie and Jolie Harden are their neighbours, and every summer host a very drunken affair to impress everyone they know.

'They're such snobs, but it's always fun.' Flo bobbed up and down. She'd mentioned the event early on in our plans.

I'm not sure she'd be quite so thrilled about my going. Ryan hates the event, but he gives in every year, and the invitation was accepted back in January.

I twiddle the invite in my hand. Well, the invite that was sent to Ryan and Flo. It's been propped on a windowsill since I arrived. The border is thick gold, and Flo giggled that the border gets thicker every year, increasing in line with Freddie's income.

Through an upstairs window, I watch the marquee go up in the Hardens' back garden. Jolie Harden, middle-aged and pumpkin-shaped, weaves through the activity. She's flapping her hands like a performing seal.

Ryan is currently loitering by their front gate. Freddie came by earlier to enlist his help. Ryan is running a palm round his neck, and lets a finger graze on unshaved stubble. Even from my viewpoint, I can see perspiration coating his skin. It's hot outside, that's for sure, and a suffocating heat haze makes it worse. For a second, I think he's going to turn round and come back inside.

I heard Freddie and Ryan's conversation earlier.

'There's some heavy lifting if you don't mind,' Freddie announced. His voice is even more plummy than Ryan's, and thick with self-importance.

'Sure. I'll come round after lunch. Do you want me to bring anything tonight? Wine? Champagne? Beer?'

Flo told me Ryan wouldn't let the side down, and that he'd still go. I had to bite back the urge to scoff when she told me he likes to stick to promises.

'No. Just bring yourself,' Freddie replied. 'Is Flo still away?'

I clicked my tongue, and waited. I learn more about Ryan through hearsay and eavesdropping than talking to him.

'Yes. Flo's still away. She'll be home soon.'

I could hear the irritation in Ryan's voice, as he'll have been willing Freddie to leave.

'Why not bring Ciara? She seems nice,' Freddie suggested.

Ryan didn't answer. I doubt he knows I inveigled my own invitation from Jolie a couple of days earlier.

Jolie had popped around. Gossip was doing the rounds. Where was Flo? Why had she left? Where had she gone? Jolie is a nosy bitch, no doubt about it. Next year, when I'm in Flo's shoes, the Hardens' is one bash that Ryan and I will not be going to.

I haven't seen Ryan face-to-face since we made out on the sofa. I've kept well out of his way, slipping in and out with the stealth of a fighter pilot. I wonder if he'll ever tell Flo what we did. Well, that's his problem. Not mine. If he does, he'll no doubt try and pass the buck the way he did with Olivia.

Poor Olivia. At least I've planned ahead, and Ryan won't be dumping me again. That's for sure.

52

CIARA

Flo told me Ryan is punctual to a fault. First at every party, always early for appointments, and hates to keep people waiting. On this knowledge, I reckon Ryan will leave the house for the garden party no later than seven o'clock.

I hang around the local park, and head back at 7.15. Cars straddle the pavement the full length of Hillside Gardens. I slink past, head down, as guests, trussed up in evening gear, spill out of Teslas, Mercedes and BMWs.

My stomach gurgles in excitement when I hear the noise coming from the Hardens' back garden. I think Glastonbury. Drink, drugs, and rock and roll. A large white board with a thick red arrow is directing guests round the side of the house. From across the road, I glimpse the host dressed in full Indian regalia, shaking hands with new arrivals. He's wearing a rich burgundy linen kurta hanging over what looks like white silk pyjama bottoms. Open-toed leather sandals wrap around glaringly white feet. Freddie obviously doesn't want guests forgetting that he worked for the British Embassy in Delhi. Jolie filled me in. I'm with Ryan, in that they're so not my type of people.

I speed up when I reach the top of the hill, and scoot inside. I've work to do, and give myself an hour tops to get ready.

I've spared no expense on preparation, and on a stunning new outfit. I got an all-over body tan, courtesy of the salon that did my nails. Flo's hairdresser was every bit as good as she said. I've had slivers of blonde highlights threaded through, and a very subtle blow-dry that seems to have increased the length of my hair. It's also twice as luscious as usual.

I'm so nervous, that I can hardly zip up my new red dress. Once I've managed, I sit under Flo's make-up light and start work on my face. Ten minutes in, I've softened fine lines with moisturiser, and foundation. I'm sparing, sticking to the subtle theme for my skin at least. My lashes seem to grow several inches with the new mascara, and with a shaky hand, I apply a final coat of red lip gloss.

I open the shoebox, and lift out my strappy new red stilettos. They're the icing on the cake. I'll worry about my empty bank account tomorrow, not tonight. Tonight is about lasting impressions.

It's 8.15 when I've finished on my make-up. I squirt Flo's really expensive perfume from her antique perfume bottle. Chanel. It's so expensive, it's choking, and my eyes sting. Then I rifle her jewellery box to find what I'm looking for.

The gold heart with a ruby in the centre, hangs on a delicate chain. It's more than perfect. I finger it longingly. It'll be mine for the night. Who knows? Maybe she'll let me keep it if I play my cards right.

I pass the landing mirror, and hardly recognise myself. If Ryan didn't recognise Mary from the nursing home, or the one-night stand from O'Malley's, he's really going to struggle tonight. The silky red dress, clings to every curve. The shoulder straps are so fine, that they slide off easily.

The last thing before I set off, is to have a well-earned drink.

The Cloudy Bay has been on chill all day. I stand, and sip steadily, until my hands stop shaking, and I feel my confidence grow. Now I need to get moving.

Let the show begin.

53

CIARA

I'm not sure about the stilettos when I enter the marquee. The heels sink into the sisal matting.

The place is buzzing, and is already packed. I spot Ryan before he spots me. He's got his back to the entrance, and is talking to a group of middle-aged men. Ryan seems to be the only one with a full head of hair.

I planned a dramatic entrance, slow, teasing, but it's slower than I'd like as my heels are hard to prise out of the matting. The men in Ryan's group look round, one by one. A small fat guy nudges Ryan.

I've aimed for the scene in *Pretty Woman*. My all-time favourite movie. I've rewound the scene in the hotel bar so many times that I'm well ready to play the part of Julia Roberts. Although, in the dim lighting, Ryan looks more handsome than Richard Gere. I wonder if he's recognised me yet.

His face grows crimson as I approach, and it'll soon be a perfect match for my dress. He leans a hand against the makeshift bar, and lifts a glass of champagne off a silver tray. From his body language, I guess he's in shock. He's soon reaching for a second glass of fizz.

'Ciara.' It's all he seems able to muster.

'Ryan. Sorry, I'm late.' I lean in and peck him on the cheek. A hint of lip gloss lingers near his jawline. I lick a finger, and wipe it off. It's as if he's seen a ghost.

'What's a girl got to do for a drink around here?'

'Let me. I'm Clayton, by the way.' The small podgy guy, face flattened like a pug's, hands me a glass of champagne, and leers. His thick hairy fingers brush against mine.

'Thanks, Clayton.'

Before I can say anything more, Ryan is seizing my arm and propelling me away from the bar. 'Excuse us please, Clayton,' he says. At least I manage to keep hold of the champagne flute.

He squeezes into a small space behind the dance floor, and pulls me in after him. We're so close, I can hear his heartbeat. It could be mine, but the tension is electric.

'Where did you get that?' He's referring to the gold heart around my neck, and starts poking at it with a really angry finger.

'It's nice, isn't it?' I'm ready for him. 'I found it in Flo's jewellery box. She'll not mind.' I finger it lovingly, tap it to my teeth.

'Keep your hands off Flo's stuff.'

Ryan's face is now claret coloured, but his anger gets muted by the din of instruments warming up.

'Chill, for goodness' sake. Can't you enjoy yourself for one evening?' I rasp throatily into his ear, letting him have a full-on whiff of Flo's perfume.

'Is that Flo's perfume?'

I'm impressed that he remembers.

'Look, let's enjoy ourselves. And...' I raise my glass '... here's to being a good sport.'

It seems to shut him up.

'Whatever,' he mumbles, and walks away.

54

CIARA

Last year, Flo stormed out early.

'Why? What happened?' I asked.

We were in the bar of Flo's guest house, putting the world to rights late one evening, when she told me all about the Hardens' garden party.

'The seating plan set things off. There were three other couples at our table. The pair next to us held hands throughout the meal. It was like a bloody séance,' she told me.

'Go on. Sounds dreadful,' I said, but it sounded fun.

'The other three couples had children, all similar ages. Then Claire Turnbull, who you'd hate on sight, asked when we were starting a family. Can you imagine?'

'Oh no. Nosy bitch.'

'Ryan took my hand, squeezed it under the table, but it didn't help. Claire asked why we didn't have kids. Did we have plans to have any. Or was I a career woman.'

As Flo told me what happened, she welled up. I put my hand over hers, as she yanked on a tissue.

'To be honest, babies just haven't happened. I wasn't ready for IVF, although Ryan was keen to try.' This part was hard to listen to.

'I was just coming round to thoughts of IVF. But then Ryan slept with Olivia.'

'I'm sorry.' What else could I say.

'I remember when I heard about Olivia, I screamed at Ryan, "If you want to play happy bloody families, then why not ask Olivia. Maybe she's pregnant."'

The dam finally burst, and Flo collapsed in floods of tears. I felt really sorry for her. If there was a moment when I might have decided not to carry out my plan, that would have been it.

Now, as I study the table plan, I see Ryan and I are seated with Claire and Mike Turnbull again. Well, I'll give Claire a thing or two to think about. Maybe I'll hold Ryan's hand under the table, and join in talk about happy families. Or perhaps I'll play footsie with Mike under the table. That should shut her up.

Either way, I'm here to enjoy myself.

* * *

When we take our seats for the meal, Ryan and I, like ace tennis players, are soon batting back questions from the other guests.

Where's Flo? Where are you from Ciara? Are you a friend of Flo's?... on and on. When Ryan rolls his eyes, smiles at me, I guess he's very drunk, or mellowing.

After dessert, Ryan heads for the cloakroom, and I excuse myself and mosey towards the bar. There's a young guy standing on his own, minus a wedding band. We manage a brief introduction, before the live band gears up for its next song. Matt, who looks all of eighteen, is young dude cool. He's hot in a bedroom-poster kind of way. Harry Styles before the cringeworthy outfits.

'Dance?' he mouths, as 'Sweet Caroline' blasts around the room. I doubt he's heard the original track, but his head bobs in time to the drumbeat. His floppy fringe covers his left eye, but he's got a great set of teeth. The whitened veneers make me think *expensive dentist.*

Over Matt's shoulder, I see Ryan approach. That's when I liven up.

'Let's go for it,' I say, grabbing Matt's hand and dragging him onto the dance floor. The dance area isn't much bigger than the spare bedroom where I'm sleeping, but the flashing lights and rainbow-coloured strobes make it feel bigger.

Matt's snake hips don't take up much room. He shuffles, as I flail my arms all over the place. Every so often he dares catch my eye. When he takes my hands, we do a together-twirl. The band leader, an ageing hippy with straggling grey hair and bare chest, lands in front of us, and holds the microphone my way.

Ryan is watching. That's for sure. He's unlooping his bow tie, stuffing it in his pocket, and ripping undone a couple of shirt buttons. Clayton whispers something in his ear, and points, before whacking Ryan on the back.

I let go of Matt, and wave my arms at Ryan.

'Come on,' I mouth. I settle my hands on my hips in mock exasperation. He does a lot of head shaking, looking all around him. Matt has stopped moving, and is like a kid who's lost his mother. He excuses himself, and slouches away.

I keep dancing. A couple of minutes, and Ryan is nudging through the throng of pear-shaped housewives and their sweaty husbands. I grab his hand.

'Hurry up. What took you so long?'

Jeez, Ryan moves even less than Matt.

'Come on. Is that all you've got?' I yell.

Suddenly, the beat slows. The husky singer breathes into a mic stuffed almost into his mouth.

'Okay, ladies and gents. Time to slow it down. Let your food digest. From Wet, Wet, Wet... "Love is All Around".'

I feel it in my fingers, I feel it in my toes...

My body is sleek with perspiration. Ryan slides one hand round my waist, and keeps a distance by holding one of my hands. He closes his eyes, inhales. I free my hand and put his around my waist.

At last, we dance as one. Our hips and bodies slide together, and he whispers, 'You smell good.'

'You too,' I say.

55

CIARA

As the music fades, Ryan disentangles his arms like one of those grab machines. The sort with shiny tentacles that slither off the prize before dumping it back on the heap.

He's already heading back to the bar before I've even straightened my dress. It's a struggle to catch up. I have to tap him on the shoulder, as he's already trying to attract the barman's attention.

'I'll be back in a mo. Off to find the loo,' I tell him.

'Fine. Whatever,' he says, and orders himself a whiskey.

I weave in and out through the milling guests. They're ill at ease, fidgety, now the music's stopped, although strobe lights are still flashing. Blue, purple, and green-coloured ice mist gets puffed out in an effort to camouflage the tackiness.

My heels sink into the soft ground, and mud sticks to my soles. A rogue hand rubs against my bottom, and fingers dig into my flesh before I slap away the balding pervert and glower at him. He's flushed from booze, and his lecherous leer tells me it's time to get out of here.

I slip out through a gap in the side of the marquee, to avoid the front of the house. As soon as I reach the street, I rip off my heels,

and scamper the short distance towards our house. *Our house.*
Mine and Ryan's.

I stand for a minute and take it all in. I'll make alterations.
We'll add a car port to the side wall. I'll make good use of my green
fingers, and have already planned the number of terracotta pots I'll
display either side of the porch. Also, the drive could do with some
tasteful ground-level lighting.

Online, I've chosen a new double-fronted door. Richly
lacquered solid mahogany. I look up. The attic can be extended
into a new bedroom. A playroom, for additions to our family.

Flo confided that she felt like a queen in her castle at the top of
their street. Once I'm finished, she'll be more Anne Boleyn than
Queen Elizabeth. That's for sure.

It's already midnight. I'm sitting on the patio looking up the
garden, and to the woods beyond.

The tacky fairy lights along the top of the fence are atmos-
pheric, rather than effective. Pretty spooky actually. I can't imagine
Ryan put the lights up, more likely Freddie Harden. He's the sort
who needs defined boundaries for his kingdom. Either way, a
really tall ladder would have been needed, and Freddie must have
an on–off switch his side as well.

The music beat from next door is still going on. It's relentless,
despite the time of night. It's like a wracking lawnmower on a
summer's afternoon. I wonder if the neighbours have
complained, but no doubt they were all asked to the party, or
bought off. Champagne, Flo told me was Freddie's favourite
sweetener.

I top up my whiskey. It stings, but tastes good. My pale blue silk
nightdress is cool against my skin, which is still burning up. I let

the fine straps hang loosely down my arms, and stretch my legs out along a wicker footrest.

I don't move, but prick my ears when I hear a noise. It's not been too long to wait. I smother a chuckle when I hear a clatter of keys. I imagine Ryan is trying to be quiet, and he might be panicking that I forgot and snibbed the door by mistake. I steady my glass, but there's more jangling before the front door opens. I left the lamp dimmed in the lounge, teasing him not to go straight upstairs.

A lull in the music, and I pick up the faint tread of shoeless feet. Ryan will have left his shoes by the front door in deference to Flo's no-shoes-in-the-house rule. Then there's the suck of bare feet over the kitchen tiles. Ryan must have noticed the fairy lights. If he wasn't so drunk, would he turn back and sneak upstairs?

I'll never know. But who cares. Problem is, Ryan can't help himself.

'Hi. I wondered where you'd gone,' he says, framed by the glass doors. One hand is stuffed in his trouser pocket, the other gripping the end of his jacket which is slung across his shoulder.

'Did you miss me?' My voice tinkles with laughter.

'Just wondered where you went.' He ignores the question.

'Fancy a nightcap? It's lovely and cool out here.'

He hooks his jacket on the doorframe, and steps out. He shivers, and falls into the seat next to me.

'Go on then. One more can't hurt,' he says. His words have a viscous slur, but they're clear enough.

I hand him an already poured generous measure. He sniffs the contents, and knocks them back in one.

'Ciara. When's Flo coming back?' he asks.

Wow. Perhaps he's not that drunk. I twirl the end of my hair with my fingers.

'Flo? To be honest, Ryan, I'm still not sure.' It's the truth. I'm not certain, although I guess it will be very soon.

'Are you in touch with her?' He stares up the garden. He sounds curious, rather than angry.

'Yes. By text.' I don't tell him that for every text I send, about twenty bounce back.

'Do you think she'll ever forgive me? I was so certain that she'd at least come home and talk. How can you be so wrong about a person?'

He certainly does great puppy-dog eyes.

'I'm often wrong about people. Even those I know best,' I say. I set my glass down, bend over. No point wasting good whiskey on being virginal.

Ryan is so sexy, and really handsome in evening clothes, but even more attractive when he's vulnerable. I feel my heart race.

'Oops. Sorry,' I say, slipping back the wispy straps that no longer contain the nightie.

It only takes a second. That's how long it takes for Ryan to decide. I wonder if I told him now that Flo would be back tomorrow, if it would make any difference. I doubt it. Ryan's a live-for-the-moment type of guy. He can't help himself.

He stretches out a hand.

'Come here, you,' he says. He pulls me over, and soon we're all mouths and tongues. His hands caress my bare skin, and he tugs the nightdress down until I'm exposed on top. Hurriedly, he unzips his trousers.

Together we let out a loud moan. The fairy lights flicker, and fade, and the music dies.

It's time to let Flo come home.

56

FLO

We roll into Bantry Bay early afternoon.

The journey down, five hours in the car, including coffee, lunch, and toilet stops, went on forever. I nodded off for a couple of hours, dizzy from the bumpy motion. Winding lanes wove back and forth, and even our destination feels like it's on the other side of the world. In this part of Ireland, we're as close as you can get to America apparently.

'Get all that sleeping out of the way,' Patrick told me. He's worn a grin from ear to ear since we left. 'We've got plenty to see.'

Patrick, a fair bit of swearing and wrong turns, finally pulls up outside an isolated cottage. If he was an axe murderer, I'd be freaking. It's in the middle of nowhere, and a couple of sheep are the only sign of life.

'I hope you're ready for this.' Patrick's face is flushed, his voice croaky. He's desperate for me to love the place. His joints creak as he gets out of the car, and he stretches out his arms and legs before yanking open my door.

'Out you get. Time to wake up.'

He hauls me out. I'm not sure what to say, as the place is so remote and the silence deafening. It makes Ballyholme look like a metropolis.

Patrick strides ahead, and turns a wobbly handle on the unlocked front door. Burglars mustn't be a threat, and when we get inside, I can see why. I follow him as he steps into the stone-floored cottage. The summer heat is instantly zapped off as if by remote control.

'Blimey. It's more basic than I remember,' he says. I'm pretty lost for words, fascinated and wary in equal measure. Patrick wanders round the single room, tugging open rickety cupboards and drawers. Apart from a fridge, a sink, a wonky table and a couple of chairs, the room is completely bare.

Patrick lifts a pint of milk from the fridge.

'Mum must have left it,' he says sniffing the carton top. 'At least we can have a cup of tea.' He rattles an old Huntley & Palmers biscuit tin, and produces a couple of tea bags. I'm not sure what to say, and giggle instead. Patrick looks aghast.

'What's so funny?'

'It's not what I was expecting, but it's...'

'It's what?' He holds the kettle under a dripping tap, and waits.

'It's amazing. I love it.' I'm not joking. It's the quiet, the isolation, and being here with Patrick. If we were on the run, it would be the perfect hideout.

'Thank God,' he says. 'I thought you might hate it.'

He fills the kettle, sets it on the gas-bottled ring, and gives me an enormous bear hug. I sink into his heat. Maybe, just maybe, things will work out okay. For both our sakes.

* * *

'Is there a shop nearby?' I ask, but I'm not holding my breath.

Both front and back cottage panoramas are of patchwork-quilt fields, and if I tried, I could count 'forty shades of green'. The only company seems to be sheep.

'About a mile. Fancy a walk?' Patrick's voice is upbeat, but his eyes haven't lost their anxious look. 'Sorry, it's a bit grimmer than I remember.'

'It's lovely. Now stop it. After London, it's heaven.'

Patrick takes my hands, raises them up and down in a relief jig.

'Let's get our bags in, and take a walk. I'll give you a proper guided tour later.'

'There's more?'

'A wee surprise round the back. That's all.'

Five minutes later we're on the dirt track that leads to the shop. The route is strewn with coffee-coloured pebbles, and dry-stone walls hold in gently rolling hills. Patrick pulls me along, his long legs setting the pace. Five hours behind the wheel, and he's chomping at the bit.

He only slows when a horse appears, whinnying through a wire fence. Patrick tugs out a handful of grass, lies it flat in his palm, and offers it to a vibrating mouth and enormous set of teeth.

'Ciara and I rode ponies to market when we were kids.'

'Oh.' I stiffen at the mention of her name.

'In those days we didn't need riding hats.'

My pursed lips don't go unnoticed.

'Sorry. I know we promised not to talk about her. I forgot for a moment.'

'You're okay. Do you like animals?'

'We grew up with them. The cottage belonged to my grandfather, and he used to own sheep, a couple of dogs, three cats and a horse.'

Patrick is at home here. That's for sure. I thread my fingers through his, stand my toes on his feet, until our faces meet. He strokes my hair, and our lips meet.

'Race you to the shop,' he suddenly whoops, plopping me back on the ground, and jogging off.

'That's not fair. Wait for me.'

We pick up fish and chips, slathered in salt and vinegar, from the village, courtesy of the shop. I don't think I've ever tasted anything as good.

The fresh air, the rugged hike, and we're ready for an early night. I've managed to turn off the fear switch for a few hours. Ballyholme, Bangor, and especially Hillside Gardens, could be on another planet.

When we get back to the cottage, Patrick shows me *the surprise* round the back. It's a small one-room guest annex, with a single bed, a sink, and a sheet of glass in the roof with a view of the stars. Patrick watches me, and I know he's hoping I'd prefer to sleep with him. But I can't, not yet. He looks pretty doleful when I say, 'It's perfect.'

'I'm next door if you get lonely.'

With that he disappears, and leaves me to stare up at the sky. His breathing soon wafts through the flimsy partition, with a soothing rhythm.

Although my body aches, and my eyelids leaden, my mind is wide awake. The turmoil is back, now I'm on my own. Patrick is so perfect. Handsome, kind, caring. Another time, another place, and we could have a future full of promise. But I'm still married.

Ryan might be a murderer, but I can't jump ship until I know why he did it. A mercy killing, or an anger killing. My insides churn, and the acid taste of vinegar coats my throat.

Freddie and Jolie Harden's party will be in full swing. As I try to name the constellations overhead, The Plough, Orion's Belt, my mind wanders. I imagine the marquee, the drunken guests, and the nauseous conversations. Ryan was right all along. I'm not sure why I ever wanted to go, but perhaps Ryan's reluctance spurred me on.

I wonder if Ryan has gone to the party, and if so, on his own. The thought that Ciara might have joined him is torture. Could they have gone together? As a couple? My stomach clenches.

It's likely Ryan made an excuse not to go. He doesn't like *false merriment*, and if he's being honest, he doesn't like being around people with more money than he has.

The sky above is a jet-black canvas, dotted with twinkling stars. I think of lying next to Ryan. His guttural snoring which has me reaching for the earplugs. I used to feel sorry for him when sleep apnoea kept him awake, as he always seemed exhausted.

Patrick is sleeping like a baby. He's at home here. I wonder if Ryan would feel at home, or be deathly bored. He's lived in England most of his life. His Irish roots were decimated by his father, the British soldier who fought terrorists, as well as Patrick's mother. Before he'd had enough and walked out.

I toss and turn. This way and that. I stretch my legs out, then hug my knees to my chest. Nothing works. The mattress is hard, but it's my thoughts that keep me awake. As I slowly slip away, the last thing I see is Ryan's mother, with her cracked lips and dried-parchment skin. I can hear her voice, the grating edge of the Northern Irish accent.

Soon I'm in the grip of a nightmare. Ryan is grasping the ends of the pillow, holding it over his mother's face. His eyes are bloodshot, and he's smiling through wet salivating lips. His horse's mouth trembles. When he lowers the pillow, and she falls silent, his fists ball in a victory clench.

As his mother's arms cease to flail, he hisses, 'Now perhaps you'll shut the fuck up.'

58

FLO

'Are you ready to meet my mother?' Patrick asks, gripping the steering wheel more tightly than usual.

'She can't be that bad. Surely?' From my experience with Irish mothers, it's hard to sound convincing.

'Come on then.'

Bronagh McCluskey's cottage is only a notch up from where we're staying. It's wider, an extra room or two, but a front garden rockery with wilting plants adds to the desolation.

I trail a couple of steps behind Patrick. He sticks his head round the front door, whistles, and then there's a screech that could wake the dead.

'Would you look what the cat's dragged in.' Patrick's mother wraps herself round him, and clings. He raises a single eyebrow at me over her shoulder, and I bite on the smirk.

When he manages to break away, Bronagh flicks back Brillo-pad hair, and wipes her hands down a gravy-splattered apron.

'Mum. This is Flo.' Patrick looks from me to his mother and back again.

'Pleased to meet you.' Bronagh's smile is colder than her voice, and I'm not sure whether to shake hands, or make a run for it. She certainly lacks her children's charm.

She doesn't wait for a reply, and lifts out a bottle of wine from another rickety fridge. It's a twin to the one in our cottage, wobbling side to side when the door is yanked.

'The bottle's already open. Here's to my boy. You do the honours.' She thrusts the bottle at Patrick, and turns back to the cooker.

'Dinner won't be long. Take Jo into the dining room if you like.'

'Flo, Mum. Not Jo.'

But Bronagh couldn't be less interested.

Out of earshot, I whisper, 'Where's the bathroom?'

'Up the stairs, and to the left.' He points towards the wooden staircase which looks as rickety as the fridge. In fact, it looks like a death trap, with a couple of missing risers halfway up. The once-white wall is peeling, and flakes of paint are scattered over the tatty stair carpet.

I manage to reach the top without falling back down, but nearly break my neck on a squishy Man U football. I flick it to one side with my foot.

There are three doors, and I feel like Goldilocks trying each handle. I quickly close the first one when I realise it must be Bronagh's room. Clothes cover the bed, the floor, a chair, and spill out from a linen basket. I assume it's a bed, but it's hard to be certain.

The next door creaks. I grit my teeth, and pause a second. The room is the size of a prison cell, but painted a rainbow of colours. There's a small bed with a blue Spiderman duvet jammed up against a wall, and a heavily inked-on school desk is slotted under a rotting window frame. Dinosaur posters are everywhere.

My pulse speeds up. My eyes race round the room, no idea what I'm looking for. Then I see it. A clue. On the inside of the door is a brightly painted name plaque. Large white letters spell one word. *LIAM*. The door frame has been defaced with ragged notches, and against each line an age has been inked in. The last one is labelled '*age 6*'.

I suddenly come over hot and dizzy. The room spins, and I dive out to find the bathroom. Once inside, I lock the door and slump against it. WTF. Bronagh McCluskey is well past child-bearing age. Then who the heck is Liam?

I splash water on my face, and lean against the sink. My mind goes into overdrive. Liam, aged six, is living here. Or perhaps he's a regular visitor. It doesn't take Poirot to work out that he must be a grandchild. But who are his parents? If he's not Patrick's, then he must be Ciara's. OMG.

'Everything okay up there?' Patrick's voice funnels up the stairs.

'Fine. Coming,' I yell. But I'm far from fine.

I wend my way slowly back down the stairs, and hear Patrick and Bronagh talking in the kitchen. From a few yards away, Patrick could be talking to Ciara. Bronagh's voice is identical to her daughter's.

How the hell am I going to sit through lunch, let alone eat anything.

59

FLO

I'm exhausted by the time we leave. If Patrick ever wants to smother Bronagh, I'll lend a hand. She's as bad as Ryan's mother was, and aimed no more than half a dozen words my way.

My mind skitters all over the place as the car bumps along. Every couple of minutes, Patrick blasts the horn on a hairpin bend, and the exhaust clanks like a death rattle. The uneven motion makes even forty winks impossible. Patrick's use of a single hand to steer doesn't help. He's caressing the steering wheel with a couple of fingers.

'Why not count sheep?' Patrick laughs. He's no idea. 'There's enough of them.'

'I'll save them for tonight.' I stare out the window. All the sheep in the world wouldn't be enough.

Liam wasn't mentioned over lunch. It was like a pact of silence between Patrick and his mother. I didn't like to ask who Liam was, as I didn't want to be caught snooping. Also, I was far from ready to hear the answer. I want to ask Patrick when we're alone.

When I first met Ciara, she called her mother a bigot, a vicious gossip, and an alcoholic gaoler. Bronagh preached that there was no escape from Bantry, and Ciara should dump the fancy notions. Hard not to sympathise with Ciara now I've been to Bantry and met her mother. Ciara showed me her eight-years-old diary. It outlined an escape plan. Think Colditz, it was that convoluted. She had drawn pictures of Cork, Belfast, London, and even one of downtown Manhattan.

'I've always wanted to be anywhere other than Bantry,' she announced.

'Shit. Bloody hell.' Patrick screams as the car swerves into a hedge, and a line of sheep amble towards us. They're bunched up, their bleats like bicycle horns.

Patrick looks mad when I laugh.

'We'll be here all night,' he snaps. He bangs his hands on the wheel as the engine cuts out.

'Would it be so bad?' I'm not sure why I ask this. Ryan would be hollering out the window by now, shaking his fists, and jamming on the horn. It's just I'm in no rush to get back.

Also the sight of the herder, with his blood-orange beanie prodding the sheep with a stick, while puffing on an e-cigarette, is one for Instagram. The guy's engulfed by vapour. I take out my phone, and snap.

'Bloody Bantry.' Patrick isn't amused, but I suddenly wonder, why all the hurry?

For fifteen minutes, until we drive on, I'm mesmerised.

If only we could stay here forever.

* * *

Patrick has calmed down by the time we reach the cottage. Dusk has fallen, and the quiet is pretty spooky. I'm not sure if it's car sickness, but I'm feeling queasy, and my insides won't settle.

'You okay?' Patrick takes my hand. 'Sorry about earlier,' he says.

'About what?'

'Yelling at the sheep.'

My smile gives him encouragement, and when we climb out he whirls me round for a kiss.

He has no idea. Or has he? He's good at deflecting contentious issues. It must be a male thing because Ryan's the master.

'Listen, go out the back and I'll get a couple of beers,' he suggests, as we trudge over the icy slabs inside the cottage.

We settle outside in the small stone-walled garden, and neck from bottles. The garden is a world away from the back of our house. A roughly hewn pond is thick with floating algae, and Patrick lights a couple of candles so that we can see each other.

Beer helps us both. It dulls my nausea, and Patrick's worry evaporates. It's like *Waiting for Godot*. The two of us sitting alone waiting. I'm waiting for answers, and Patrick's dreading the questions. Neither of us is willing to break the silence.

We sit side by side, looking towards the east. I should be angry at Patrick for not being honest. Not telling me about Liam, whoever Liam is. But is omission lying? It is with Ryan because he usually has an agenda to save his own skin. Patrick is different. He's scared the truth will destroy *us*, and any chance of a future together.

'Hit me,' Patrick says. 'What's bothering you?'

'Who is Liam?'

Patrick takes his time. He must have known this would be my first question, but maybe he didn't hear me upstairs going into Liam's room. Okay, I'm grasping at straws.

'He's Ciara's son. Ciara pays Mum to look after him. No one knows who the father is, but abortion was illegal when she got pregnant. She had no choice but to have him. He's a great wee lad.'

'Where was he today?' I gulp the beer and watch as foam cascades on to the ground.

'With his aunt. Mum's sister, Mairead, helps out.'

'Does Liam know Ciara is his mother?'

'Yes. She promises, on her rare visits, that one day she'll come and get him.'

'What's she waiting for?'

I roll the empty beer bottle across the ground until it bangs against the wall.

'Are you sure you're okay?' A deep ridge nestles between Patrick's eyebrows.

How do I answer him? That my life is in ruins. And I'm wondering if my husband might be the father to a son he's never heard about.

Oh my God. Unless... Ciara has already told him.

Patrick sits on the edge of his seat, and fidgets. He looks distraught. I'm not sure how much he's picking up on, or how much he might already know. I guessed Liam was Ciara's son, but it's still a shock hearing Patrick say the words.

'Let me keep you warm.' Patrick tries to coax me on to his lap. 'You've got goosebumps all along your arms.'

I take a deep breath.

'If you don't mind, I think I'll turn in. We've got an early start, and I don't know about you, but I'm knackered.' I exaggerate a yawn, knowing there's little chance of sleep.

'No worries.' He looks so miserable.

Patrick is unlike Ciara in so many ways, and maybe I give him the benefit of the doubt because he's hot, and he's a guy.

Is he really so different? He's withheld the truth from me, twice. He didn't own up about Ciara being his sister, until he had no other choice. And now there's Liam. Why didn't he tell me weeks ago? Maybe it would have made me think twice about letting Ciara have the keys to my life.

Does Patrick suspect Liam might be Ryan's? Then again, how

could he? Unless Ciara told him, and they're in on some sort of scam together.

Once we've said goodnight, and Patrick's door is closed, I lie down on the lumpy mattress, and let the tears roll. I've got no one in the world I can trust. Even if my parents were still alive, I'm not sure how much I could tell them. I sob silently until I'm all dried up.

As clouds roll across the sky and block out the stars, I get an inkling of a plan. It's loosely formulated, but it's taking shape.

If Ciara is playing a dangerous game, she is seriously underestimating the opposition.

60

FLO

Patrick and I don't talk much on the journey home. We leave early, and it's almost lunchtime by the time we pull up outside the guest house.

Patrick looks forlorn.

'I'll call later,' I tell him, leaning back in through the passenger window.

'Please. And, Flo... thanks for coming.'

'It was fun.' I'm not sure what else to say. If there had been no Liam, no Ciara, no Ryan, it would have been really fun.

'I need to get back, talk to Ryan. Get my head sorted.'

'I know. I'm patient.' He manages a winsome smile.

'Sorry,' I say.

As I walk up the steps to the guest house, I feel his eyes following me. I turn and blow him kisses.

'Love you,' he mouths through the window, as he rubs a finger in the corner of an eye. I must be mad. Another time, another place, Patrick would be my perfect match. I'll really miss him. My own eyes smart with tears, but till death us do part... I'm still married to Ryan.

I wave as Patrick drives off, black smoke billowing from his exhaust.

I dump my overnight bag in my room, and before I book my flight back to Luton for tomorrow, I've got one last visit to make.

I set off in the direction of Bangor, and nineteen minutes later, I reach my destination. A small pebble-dashed semi-detached. The front wall of the property is less than two yards from the house, and a rotting wooden bench is slotted into the gap. Flowerpots, thick with weeds, cluster round the door. The net curtains twitch as I push through the gate.

Mrs Harrison has been waiting for me since my call. She wasn't hard to find, as Mr Connor told me exactly where she lived, and even managed to locate a phone number.

'Hard to hide out in Bangor, everyone knows your business,' he said.

I lift my hand to knock, but the door opens before I've a chance.

'Mrs Harrison?' I ask.

'That's me, aye. Come in. I've been watching for you. Flo, I think you said?'

'Yes. That's right.'

I reckon Mrs Harrison is in her eighties. Wispy white hair crinkles like tissue paper on a translucent scalp. A small dowager's hump pokes through a shiny nylon blouse, and as I follow her through to the lounge, I notice her left foot drags.

'We'll sit in here. It's nice and warm,' she says. I shiver, wondering at our differing ideas of warm. A one-bar electric fire beams with futile effort.

'Thank you.'

'Cup of tea? I've put the kettle on.' She's already heading for the kitchen.

'Please. Milk, two sugars.'

The top of a dark wooden sideboard is cluttered with pictures. I lift one with three people in it.

'Just waiting for the kettle to boil.' Mrs Harrison's voice makes me jump. 'That's Gerald, my late husband, and our son Bill,' she says. 'I've lost them both, you know.'

'I'm really sorry.' Of course I know. That's the reason I'm here.

She hobbles off again, and returns a minute later with a tray. A teapot, two china mugs, a sugar bowl and a milk jug are part of a matching set. She sets the tray down, and goes back a third time for a plate of buttered scones.

We sit on threadbare maroon armchairs, and my back is plumped up by cushions with crocheted covers.

Mrs Harrison's hand wobbles as she passes me a cup.

'That picture was taken a few years before Gerald died.' She takes the picture from me, kisses the glass.

'It must be lonely for you,' I say.

'I can't forgive him,' she says. 'Bill, that is. My son.' She clears her throat of phlegm and puts a hand to her heart. She's trying hard not to cry.

'Suicide is really upsetting for those left behind,' I say, sipping the lukewarm tea. Slowly her wheezing subsides.

'It wasn't the suicide I can't forgive.' She gives her head a violent shake.

'Oh. What was the problem? What couldn't you forgive?'

When I called Mrs Harrison from the guest house, I told her I wanted to talk to her about the death of her husband at Mulberry Lodge. At that stage I didn't mention suicide, or her son, Bill.

Since learning that Ciara worked at Mulberry Lodge when both Ryan's mother and Gerald Harrison died, I've had a hunch that I'm missing something. When old newspaper cuttings flagged up the suicide of Gerald's only son, Bill, not long after his father's death, I got a queasy feeling. Had Ciara had any part

in Bill Harrison's suicide? It's a long shot, but the suspicion i
there.

'Bill. He was having an affair.' Mrs Harrison spits the words
and saliva spots her blouse. 'Some fancy piece working at the
nursing home.'

I pull my horror face. 'Who with?' I ask. Shit. I know what she's
going to say.

'That bloody wee tart, Mary McCluskey.'

Ciara having an affair with a balding middle-aged man? Could
I have got her that wrong? No. That's not her style. Even if she was
being paid.

'I never told the police. Bangor's a gossipy place, and I've kept it
to myself. But I've got the proof right here. I dug it out for you.'

She points to a drop-leaf table, strewn with papers. I wander
over, and begin leafing through the pile, which is mainly made up
of bank statements. The first statement is dated two weeks after
Bill's father died. My finger runs down the columns. Black rings
have been inked round different figures. Regular payments were
withdrawn each month thereafter. Three hundred pounds the first
month. Then £400, and rising to £500 over the course of the first
year.

'He was paying his bloody fancy woman. For her services, no
doubt. A right prostitute that one.'

As a cough convulses Mrs Harrison's body, I rearrange the
statements in a neat pile.

Who am I to tell her that these were likely blackmail payments
Ciara extorted to keep her quiet about Bill killing his father? Better
a philanderer than a killer. It's not my place to tell her.

'Bill squandered the legacy his father left him. Bill always said
he'd move out when his dad died, buy himself his own little place.
But instead he paid for sex. God in heaven help us all.' She does

the sign of the cross, and finally opens the floodgates. Tears pour down her cheeks.

I hug her on my way out, thank her for the tea and scones.

'Thank you for coming. I'm lost for company,' she says, and closes the door after me.

This is the moment I decide. I'll definitely be going through with my plan.

61

CIARA

Ryan sobers up pretty quickly after we've had sex. He's certainly not one for pillow talk.

'I'll head up,' he says. 'And thanks.'

He really thinks he's just going to slink off.

'What for?'

He's now lost for words. If he thinks he's going to get away with skulking upstairs, he's got it all wrong.

'Everything,' he says. He checks his trouser zip, and picks up his jacket.

'Hasn't anything come back to you?' I follow a few inches behind him as he slouches into the kitchen.

'What? Hasn't what come back to me?' he snaps, desperate to get away. Well, not so fast.

'Remember the day your mother died. Don't you remember popping into O'Malley's pub for a few drinks?'

'Go on.' He puts a supporting hand against the table, and tries to work out where I'm coming from.

'Don't you remember the woman you picked up at the bar?'

He blinks several times, as if it'll help clear his head. Both hands are now leaning on the table, and his jacket has fallen on the floor.

'What woman?'

'Listen, I'm not Flo. You don't need to lie to me. I'll fill you in. The woman you made love to in the back of a hire car, and then ghosted.'

His legs seem to buckle, and he collapses into a chair.

'That was you?' His eyes widen in disbelief. 'I thought you worked at the nursing home.'

'Yep. The very same. I worked at the nursing home during the day, but I also had a social life. Of sorts.'

'You're fucking joking me.' His voice is raspy, and he's having trouble getting out his words.

'Nope. I'm not.'

I pull out another chair, turn it to face him.

'What is it you want? Why are you here?' he asks.

'Let's just say, we've got unfinished business. And don't you think we're good together?'

I stretch out a hand, lay it on his thigh, but he rears out of his chair, knocks it across the room, and smashes his fist into a wall. There's an almighty crack, before he goes quiet. For a moment, I think he's going to go for me.

He comes closer and spits in my face, 'Listen, whoever you are. I want you out of my house. Now.'

'Look. No hard feelings, it's all water under the bridge. I'll not tell Flo, promise. It'll be our little secret.'

'You bet it'll be our little secret.'

As he storms out, my whole body starts to shake. Maybe I shouldn't have told him, but I don't think secrets will work for us. He needs to hear the whole story.

The only thing I want from Ryan is him. He's been my fantasy for so long. I could blackmail him for what he did to his mother, to get what I want. But I'd rather he chose me over Flo, all by himself. I want her life, her husband and her home.

As I turn off the lights, lock up, I decide I need to give Ryan space. Tomorrow, I'll move a few things into the pub. Flo will be back soon, and once she works out what Ryan's been up to, I doubt she'll hang around.

I'm depending on it.

62

CIARA

It's Monday, and I haven't seen Ryan since Saturday night. I've kept well clear. He needs time to calm down, work things out.

I've done both the early and late shifts at the pub. I've been run off my feet, with regulars and sweaty darts teams. There's been little time to wallow, think about things, and by closing time I'm still buzzing.

The pub is nearly empty. Bonzo, the landlord, is draped across the counter, facing a young girl with fish-pout lips, scary tattooed eyebrows, and orange skin. She swivels unsteadily on a bar stool, and Bonzo keeps topping up her drink.

I watch as he places a large hand over hers, and something he says makes her burst out laughing. I could be looking at myself. I'm fearful for the girl, as it hasn't taken me long to get the measure of the landlord.

Bonzo motions me over, and asks me to clear glasses, and help stack chairs onto the tables.

'Carrie, can you finish off here?' He still hasn't got my name right. 'I'll be back in about half an hour, and then you can clock off. Well done.' Bonzo slaps me on the bottom, and burps in sync.

I fill the dishwasher, and hear the landlord climb the back stairs, followed closely by the girl. Her laughter has toned down and soon abates completely.

I shut up shop, bolt the doors and windows, and tiptoe up to the first-floor landing. From the grunting and groaning, I suspect the landlord won't be as long as half an hour.

I make it back to the bar just in time before the couple reappear.

'I'll be off now, boss,' I say.

'When are you moving in?' he asks. 'Your room's ready.' He smiles, tugging down his several-sizes-too-small T-shirt over his bloated paunch.

'In a day or two,' I say. 'See you tomorrow.'

The drunken girl has collapsed in the corner of the lounge with her head slumped on top of folded arms. She sobs uncontrollably, and the noise follows me onto the street.

I take the longer route back to the house, skirting through side streets to avoid the main road. It's cold out, but fresh after the pub, and I gulp greedily at the night air, letting it disinfect my body from the stench of stale ale.

I dig out my phone and there's a new message from Flo. I lean up against a lamppost.

I'll be back this week. Have your bags packed. F.

She's about a week too late. Wait till she finds out what her husband has been up to.

See you soon! C.

I keep it simple, and press 'send'. Even if Flo leaves Ryan, and tries to take him to the cleaners, Ryan and I should have enough. He earns a good salary, and with my bar work, we should be okay.

However, just in case, I'll hold on to my independence, and carry on with my sideline. Tomorrow, when I get the chance, I'll install a small video recorder in Bonzo's bedroom. If I'm right, he's taken more than one young girl up there for after-hours drinks.

I know his sort, and the type of girls he preys on. I was once one of those girls.

And people like him deserve to pay.

63

FLO

My knuckles grip the seat belt, and I lean my face against the cool of the porthole. The seat belt sign is on, and the aircraft engines are ready for take-off. I'm a nervous wreck.

I miss the comfort of Ryan's hand. I grip ferociously whenever the plane begins to taxi, and my anxious fingers gouge divots in his smooth tanned skin.

'Ouch,' he grimaces, embracing the pain, pleased to be of help. But when he falls into a deep sleep once we're up, I fidget on the edge of my seat, my toes sore from curling. A couple of drinks take the edge off, but today I can't risk a drink. I need to keep a clear head.

Before I turn my phone to Airplane Mode, I reread Ryan's last three texts.

Flo

You need to get in touch. Please. I need to know what's going on. It's a nightmare with Ciara here.

This was sent at two o'clock the morning. After the Hardens' garden party.

At 2.30, another message.

Flo

Please come home. We can sort this mess out. I'll do whatever it takes. XX

The final message was sent at 2.55.

Flo

Please get in touch. WE NEED TO TALK

He must have been very drunk. It's the second time he's sent panicky texts in the early hours.

I finally key in a response.

Ryan

I'm on my way back. See you soon.

I don't say when, even though I know he hates surprises. But I think he'll be glad to see me.

Through the small aeroplane window, the Northern Irish countryside, a patchwork quilt of green ragged squares, their edges marked by stone walls, clipped hedges, and random fencing, floats beneath the buffeting craft. I let out a little yelp as the plane hits the grey band of clouds, before it levels out.

The short fifty-five-minute journey, the same time it takes Ryan to commute from our house to his office in London, transports me between two completely different worlds. The Irish Sea divides cultures defined both by geography and history. Discontent rumbles in the Irish provinces, tethered by religious fetters. But in

England, the chains have been unlocked and life rages chaotically. I'm no longer sure which world I prefer.

The plane banks as it descends towards Luton Airport. Life is already speeding up. A twinge of nostalgia for Bantry, the clear air, smiling faces and easy pace of life have left their mark. Who knows? Perhaps I'll return, one day. But as I squeeze my eyes tight for landing, I block out all thoughts, except of getting down and getting home.

* * *

I hurry through arrivals at Luton Airport, and grab a taxi, asking to be dropped off at the top of Mount Street. Fifteen minutes from home.

When we get there, the driver plonks my bag on the pavement, and speeds off. You can tell I'm back in England. I shield my eyes against the sun, and look down the hill. I can only just make out the sign of the Winterton Arms swaying on chains, some thirty or forty yards further on.

Although Ryan and I only once ventured inside the pub, we've passed it enough times when out jogging. It's at the bottom of the hill, near the start of our regular route, and Ryan would yell at me to keep up as we tackled the incline.

'Come on, Flo. Give it some effort. Push, push.' Ryan would jog on the spot, his tight calves straining to go faster. Six London marathons, and one New York, sets Ryan apart from the fun-runners. He doesn't do things for fun, it's all about competition and proving his worth. I think it started with trying to prove his mother wrong, as she had him believe he was useless. Like his father.

I wipe the back of my hand across my eyes, to clear the mixture of sweat and tears.

Lunchtime drinking should be nearly over. I guess Ciara will ɔe cleaning tables, polishing optics rather than flirting with ːustomers. Too early in the day even for her.

I straighten my shoulders, grip the handle on my case, and narch down the hill. My head is light from lack of food and ɪerves, but determination is feisty fuel. My weapon today is the ≥lement of surprise.

Ciara has no idea what's about to hit her.

64

CIARA

I'm not in the mood to hang around. Bonzo insists I clear up, and shouldn't leave until the place is spotless, ready for the night shift.

Everyone's left, and the silence is bliss. I squint through the half-empty bottle of house wine, jiggle it up and down, and pour out the dregs. I'm about to take a sip when the door springs opens.

'We're closed,' I yell.

'Hello, Ciara.'

The glass slips from my hand, and I freeze. Flo is standing right behind me, I can see her in the bar mirror. She's dressed in skinny jeans, and trademark floaty blouse. Her hair is hanging loose, straighter than usual, as if it's been ironed out. She looks different. Maybe it's the skew from the mirror, but she looks menacing, no hint of a smile.

'Oh my God! Flo. You gave me a shock.' I swivel too fast, and have to steady myself on the counter. 'It's soooo good to see you.'

I push up the bar hatch, squeeze through, and fling my arms wide. She doesn't move a muscle, just looks me up and down.

'Nice to see you too, Ciara. You're looking good.' The sarcasm is aimed at my working garb. I rub wet hands down my black trousers, and whip off the scrunchie from my hair. I couldn't look any worse.

'Can I get you a drink? Wine? Prosecco?'

'No, you're okay. A coffee would be good though.'

Flo looks round the bar, a full 360.

'A long time since I was in here. Hasn't improved much,' she says, before wheeling her case over to one of the tables.

'Here. Give me a mo, and I'll wipe it down.' I grab a damp cloth, wring it till my knuckles sting.

'I guessed this was where you were working when you sent through the picture.'

'It's only a stopgap.' I rub hard at the stale beer rings, but they're ingrained.

'Oh. You're not going back to Ireland?'

'Not right away.' I fling the cloth back on to the bar. 'Cappuccino?'

'That'll do nicely. Plenty of milk, you know how I like it.'

'Coming up.'

I loiter by the machine, grinding my teeth and the beans at the same time. In the glass, I watch her. She's fiddling with a gold chain around her neck. It's the one I suggested Patrick buy her, with the two interlocking gold harps. The sight of the chain helps me relax. Perhaps she and Patrick have got closer.

The milky coffee dribbles onto the saucer as I set it down in front of her.

'Oops. Sorry.'

She's already torn open a couple of sugar sachets, and is stirring furiously.

'I'll get myself a drink, and we can catch up. I'm dying to hear about Patrick.' I force a laugh. I need to stay calm but my heart's in my mouth and my legs like jelly. It's as if she's here to arrest me. She's too bloody calm.

I sit down opposite her, and lift my wine in the air. If she doesn't, I certainly need more than coffee.

'Cheers.' I take a large mouthful. 'Where to start.'

She simply smiles, eyes skimming over the rim of her mug.

Why has she suddenly appeared? Is she back to forgive Ryan? Tell him it's all over?

I wonder if he knows she's back. The thought makes my insides clench.

At least I've got a place to stay. But holy shit.

65

FLO

I wonder why Ciara is so surprised. Did she think I'd never come back?

I want her to feel really uncomfortable, and not to guess what I'm thinking. She'll find out all in good time.

She's acting as if nothing's happened, that she hasn't nearly destroyed Ryan's and my lives. I need to stay calm, and stick to the plan. But it's really tough, seeing her face to face.

I use a spoon, scoop out the last of the milk.

'Are you off?' she asks.

'Yep. I need to get *home*.' I emphasise the word home, then sling my handbag over my shoulder. 'Oh, and while I'm here, can I have my phone back. House and car keys too.'

Her face is a picture. For someone so conniving, she's lagging well behind.

'Shit. I think I left your phone at home. Not allowed to use it at work.' Her cheeks redden, but she's soon scurrying over to the bar.

I dig out the cheap pay-as-you-go mobile, and ring my iPhone. Does she think I'm that stupid? As if she'd leave her phone at home. She'll be keeping tabs on Ryan, monitoring messages and calls every few minutes.

'Oh. I must have it with me after all.' Ciara bangs a smile in place when 'Air on the G String' rings out. Strange, I thought she'd have changed the ringtone.

It takes her a further minute to locate the house and car keys. As I put them in my pocket, I hand her the burner phone.

'There's a little data left, but not much.' I squeeze the mobile into her palm.

I then bite the bullet. 'Listen. Why not come round for supper. A last supper of sorts.' I manage a smile. No eyes. Mouth only.

'Sure. What sort of time?' She's no idea why I've asked her round. I doubt she'll think it's to say: A*ll is forgiven. A great joke.* She fiddles with a pile of bar mats, stacks them then spreads them out again.

'Seven okay?'

She nods.

'Great. See you then,' I say, already walking away.

By the door, I raise an arm, trill my fingers. I know she's watching.

* * *

Outside in the sunshine, I lean against the pub wall, and let all the pent-up air explode. I have to brace myself to check the phone. Odd, Ciara hasn't changed the passcode either. I thought it would have been the first thing she did. It's certainly a miscalculation on her part, but it looks as if she really had no idea I was about to turn up.

I scroll through recent messages between Ciara and Ryan. They certainly tell a story, but a story that's in the past. I delete them all, and send a new message.

What time will you be back? I'm doing rabbit stew. Hope you're
hungry. X

Now to get home. Take my life back, my possessions, and most
importantly my husband. Tomorrow I'll arrange for a locksmith to
come round.

One last stop. The butcher's to pick up the rabbit.

I'm expecting Ryan home anytime. He only responded to the text asking what time he would be back, about twenty minutes ago.

I'm on the way. Rabbit stew sounds good.

The message, and lack of kisses confirms my assumption that he thought the original text was from Ciara.

The view from the kitchen window is an amazing vantage point. I told Ciara where to stand to get a great view down the street. Callers can't see in unless they come up close and stick their noses to the glass. It's like a police mirror. Good guys on one side, baddies on the other.

Funny, when Ryan walks the incline, he invariably looks down. Could be he wants to avoid conversation with the neighbours, but tonight he's stooped even lower than usual.

He hesitates by the Hardens', and stares at something in our drive. The Audi. Ciara had left the car parked askew, and perhaps he's noticed it's been re-parked.

'Why don't you measure the distances?' Ryan suggested when

would re-park the car several times. I like it straight. Well, straight to the eye. He laughed when I stormed inside, dug out a tape measure and did exactly that. I chalked out a parking bay in the tarmacked section of the front drive. The rain soon washed it away, but I would mark it out at least once a week, and it was the first thing I did today when I got back.

Ryan is gripping a carrier bag. It's from the Wine Shoppe at the end of our road. Perhaps he's restocking on the Cloudy Bay. There's only one bottle left. I try and nudge back the assumptions that he's bought wine for him and Ciara.

I turn up the music speaker, and hum along to 'The Streets of London'.

How can you tell me, you're lonely?
And say for you that the sun don't shine

It's my karaoke favourite. He's in the drive, the front door is open, so he'll hear the music. That must be why he's hovering again.

I keep my eyes directed through the window, my back to the door. I wonder if he'll twig straight away that I'm not Ciara. My hair's longer, straighter than when I left, and I've added a few high-lights. From the back, Patrick says Ciara and I could be mistaken, save for his sister's extra two inches in height. I've put on a pair of kitten heels to plug the difference. Ryan hates surprises, but hope-fully today, I'll be a welcome one.

'Hi,' he says. I go rigid at his voice. It's as if he's crept up and booed.

'Hi, Ryan. Good to see you.'

'Flo? Oh my God. Is it really you?'

The carrier bag slips from his grasp, and a bottle falls out, smashing onto the tiles.

'You're back. I can't believe it.'

He looks in total shock, his voice as wobbly as his appearance. He looks down at the clear liquid oozing across the floor, and grips tightly onto a second bottle. He takes it out, plops it down on the table. Pinot Grigio, my favourite. The label on the broken bottle is turned up, it's a Sauvignon Blanc. Mud House. Ciara's favourite. In Ballyholme, she stocked up on Mud House because it was always on offer at the local Co-Op.

'Welcome home. Oh my God. You don't know how great it is to see you.' He stares as if I've risen from the dead.

'It's good to be home. Here, I'll clear up. You go and change. And...' I inch towards him, sidestepping the glass and slime, 'What about a welcome home kiss?'

'Of course. I wasn't sure...' His voice fades, and he is suddenly squeezing the air out of me. His lips linger on top of my head, and gently he lowers his lips.

'Okay. That's enough.' I laugh, perhaps a bit too loudly, but so what. I've never seen Ryan so happy. 'You get changed, and supper's nearly ready.'

'Shall I open the wine for you?' He holds up the Pinot Grigio, turns the label my way. His face suggests he's won the lottery.

'No need. A bottle is already open.'

It's a few seconds later that he notices the table settings. There's three of everything. Three full sets of cutlery. Three cut-glass crystal wine flutes, red serviettes folded inside. Three side plates, and even three bread rolls. It will be the last time the table is set for three. Three people in a marriage is one person too many.

'Who's coming for supper?' His happy face evaporates.

'Who do you think?' I roll my eyes. It's a sneaky surprise, but I want to watch them together.

'I won't be long,' he says, and shuffles out.

67

FLO

I've never been one to crave control. I've always let Ryan think he has the upper hand.

Since we got married, I've humoured him, even when he over-does the sarcastic put-downs. I know it helps him feel better about himself, and his put-downs are always verbal. He's never laid a finger on me, although he's come close. A couple of times he raised a hand, and I had to back off. Recently, I've wondered what might have happened if I'd kept at it. I don't dare think about it.

I've always been so in love that I've let Ryan get away with murder. Literally, as it turns out. Yet no matter what he's done, I'm always the first to apologise, and play things his way. I've always played Jane to his Tarzan.

Going forward, I need to set new ground rules, and make Ryan think twice about things he says, and does. I doubt he'll try and play me again any time soon, and if he really wants our marriage to work, he'll have to accept we're equal partners. Once he knows I've seen what he did to his mother, he should be much more pliable.

As I rearrange the herb pots, straighten the toaster and kettle, and position the knife rack, the salt and pepper cellars, and the olive oil at right angles to the wall, my mind mulls over, for the umpteenth time, whether Ryan will have seen the videos yet. I sort of doubt it.

Since I learned about Liam, I imagine Ciara's not in such a rush to make a move. As far as I know, no one other than Ciara and I know what Ryan did to his mother, but I guess I'm the only one who really understands why he did it. I need him to tell me himself, open up, so that we can lay her ghost to rest.

Tonight will be the first night of the rest of our lives. I'll play a little game of poker round the dinner table, but once Ciara's out of our lives, Ryan and I have work to do at rebuilding our marriage. And most importantly, the trust.

This evening I need to hold in check my fury with Ciara. I'm not one to hate, but she's pushed me to my limits. Once we kick her out, I never want to set eyes on her again.

While I'm waiting for Ryan to come down, and for Ciara to turn up, I wander out to the patio with a large glass of chilled Pinot Grigio. The strong smell of rabbit stew wafts after me.

The pot plants have all been watered. I wonder if it was Ryan or Ciara who did the nurturing. Ryan leaves what he calls 'the pretty-ing' of the garden to me. Maybe my absence has made him realise how much I do when he's at work. There's no doubt someone has been looking after the garden, feeding the geraniums, and herbs since I've been away.

If Ryan had his way, he'd rip out all the random bushes, get rid of the flowerbeds that run under the fencing, and rip up the lawn. Before I left, the one thing we agreed on was the latter. We agreed to take up part of the lawn, and build a small, eco-friendly decking area. Ryan was to lead the project, and it's the first thing I'd like him to tackle now I'm back.

I don't hear Ryan come up behind me, and I would have literally hit the roof if I wasn't outside.

'Don't creep up like that. You scared me to death.'

Ryan laughs. He used to love creeping up on me.

'Fancy some company?' He holds his beer bottle against my glass. 'Cheers.'

'Cheers,' I echo. His smile gets even broader.

'The garden's looking good,' I say.

'It's given me something to do. Flo, I'm so glad you're home. You've no idea.'

Actually, I've a pretty good idea.

'I'm glad to be back,' I say.

'You are here to stay, aren't you?'

I nod, and his shoulders visibly unravel.

'I presume it's Ciara coming to dinner?' It's a rhetorical question, but he tenses in the asking.

'Who else? She's part of the furniture. But don't worry, it'll be the last time.'

We stand side by side. Husband and wife, but with the awkwardness of first-time lovers.

'Flo, Ciara needs to leave. Now you're back she has to go.'

'Don't worry. I've already told her. She's coming to pick her things up and move into the pub.'

Ryan slops into a garden chair. At the same moment the Hardens' cat appears, wobbling along the top of the fence, and bounds boldly onto the lawn in front of us.

'Here, Zippy. Puss, puss, puss.' I click my fingers, repeat the chorus until the cat saunters over, tail heavenwards. A loud, soothing purr rumbles in the quiet of evening. I rub my hand along her soft ginger fur until she rolls over, teasing me towards her stomach.

'Be careful. She'll bring you out in a rash,' Ryan warns.

Before I answer, there's a loud rap on the front door and Zipp
scoots off. Time stands still.

'Shall I get that?' Ryan asks.

'You're okay. I'll go.'

I'm already on my feet.

68

CIARA

I lock up as soon as Flo leaves the pub.

I charge up the High Street to the O2 phone shop. The cheap burner phone which Flo tossed at me, has only one bar of battery, and no data. By the time I've topped up, bought a charger, it's almost four. I perch on a wooden bench, swivel the phone in the air until I get a signal.

Flo turning up at the pub has thrown me. I certainly wasn't ready for her, and have no idea what her plans are. Is she back to make up with Ryan? Have things moved on with Patrick, and is she going to throw Ryan out?

I'm so cold, yet the sun is high in the sky, not a cloud in sight. My fingers skitter across the screen.

'Patrick? It's me.' The line crackles, fizzles in and out.

'Flo? I can hardly hear you. Where have you been? I've been really worried.'

'It's Ciara.' I raise my voice, snapping out the words.

'Ciara? Christ the line's dreadful. Why are you on Flo's phone? That's her new number, isn't it?'

'Never mind that. Listen, Flo's back in England. Did you know she was coming back?'

'I knew she was heading that way, but haven't heard since she left. I can't get hold of her. Is everything okay?'

Patrick is panicky, I hear it in his tone. He's preparing for the worst.

'How much does she know?' I ask

'About what?'

'Us.'

A car pulls up alongside the kerb, and blasts its horn. I scowl, and slap a palm over one ear. I wait till the driver roars away, and make an obscene gesture.

'Sorry, Patrick. What did you say?'

'It sort of slipped out.'

'What slipped out?'

'That we're brother and sister.'

'Go on. Does she know about Liam?'

'We went to Bantry for the weekend, had lunch with Mum. Yes, she knows about Liam.'

'How much?'

'That he's six and the result of a drunken one-night stand. What else could I tell her?'

'What was her reaction?'

'Surprised, that was all. What's this all about? And when are you coming back? Jimmy's pestering to see if he needs to find a new barmaid.'

'I'll let you know. By the way, how are you and Flo getting on? Is it serious?'

'I like her. A lot. That's all I'll say for now.'

'Listen, I must go. Take care, and speak soon.' I disconnect. I think I've heard enough.

* * *

I wend my way through the park, as it's too early to get changed. I turn my face towards the sun, but I still can't get warm. I rub my hands up and down my arms, blow into cupped hands.

How much has Flo worked out? Has she guessed Liam is Ryan's son? How could she though, unless Ryan owned up to what he did, which is unlikely. Liam is my trump card if Ryan finds it hard to choose between Flo and me. I'm the only one who knows for certain that Liam is Ryan's.

Since I met Ryan, and then Flo six years later, my plan for the perfect life has taken shape. I've been dreaming of it since I was Liam's age. With Ryan by my side, I can have it all. A beautiful home, kids, and a man I can't get enough of.

A little smile creeps in. I've actually got two trump cards. Ryan shouldn't be so trusting. Flo might have seen Ryan murder his mother, but she definitely hasn't heard her husband fuck the houseguest.

69

CIARA

It's one minute to seven by the time I reach the top of Hillside Gardens.

The front of the house is in shadow. The Audi is tightly tucked in to the right angle between the front and side wall, and all the windows in the house are closed. The cul-de-sac is eerily quiet, no sign of life anywhere. If it wasn't for the car, and the fact I'd been invited, I'd think there was no one at home.

My finger lingers over the doorbell. I wonder if Ryan is home. What if he isn't back from work, or isn't coming at all? I push my ear against the door, but there's no sound from inside. I stab at the bell, three or four times. When there's no reply, I rap firmly with the brass knocker. I peer through the frosted panel, until Flo's image floats into view. It's distorted, and I step back half expecting her to appear through the glass.

I stumble back down the steps when the door flies open. Flo flings her arms wide, thrusts herself up against the wall, and with a sweeping gesture ushers me in.

'Come in. Come in,' she says.

'Hi. Hope I'm not late.' It's exactly seven, but it's an opener.

I slip off my sandals and place them neatly by the hall table. Flo's kitten heels bring her up almost to my height. I'm surprised she's allowing shoes in the house, but then she makes the rules.

There's no attempt at air-kissing. If she recognises the Mint Velvet dress, she doesn't comment. She's so many clothes in her wardrobe, she might not twig. It's the sort of floaty thing she likes to wear, and Ryan seems to like. On a wife, although perhaps not on a sexy mistress.

'Perfect timing,' she says. 'Come on through.'

I grip the bottle of Pinot Grigio, but my hands are so sweaty I have to put a palm under the base to steady it.

'We're having drinks in the garden. You know where that is, I presume.' Flo forces a laugh. 'Ryan's out there. You've met him already, I think.'

I look down at my bare feet and red-painted toenails which look as if they're covered in blood. Flo didn't mention we were going outside, but frozen feet are preferable to retreating down the hall.

There's a strong smell in the kitchen. Overpowering, but familiar. It takes me a moment to work it out.

'Something smells good,' I say. 'Rabbit stew?'

'What else?' Flo lets out another exaggerated puff of amusement, as she lifts the casserole lid up and down, and flaps away the steam.

She's really edgy, tightly strung, but hard to read. My heart races, and my stomach somersaults as I step outside.

'Ciara.' Ryan looks at me uncomfortably.

'Hi,' I say. I'm not sure where to sit. There are only two chairs pulled close together, and Ryan doesn't get up.

Ryan slugs from a bottle, his eyes unfocused. His hair hasn't been combed, and the bags under his eyes are so black, he's hard to recognise. But he's my man. When he runs a hand through lank fringe, I have an urge to lean over and do it for him.

I opt to sit on the low parapet wall rather than the chair in cas Flo appears with a meat cleaver. My feet jiggle to get circulation, a they could be immersed in ice.

When Flo appears, Ryan looks sharpish in her direction. H pats the empty seat, and pulls the chair even closer to his own.

He then takes Flo's hand and rests it on his lap.

The Irish are good at small talk, but even I'm struggling. Ryan efforts involve mention of Irish versus English weather, footbal results, and mortgage rates. If it wasn't so cold we'd all be aslee Flo doesn't say anything, doesn't interrupt, but fiddles with Ryan fingers as if they're antique finds.

Ten minutes in, and Flo announces the food should be read She hops up, and with a click of kitten heels leads the way.

'Ladies first.' Ryan nods for me to follow.

It's bizarre, like a ménage à trois getting acquainted. Flo ha overdone the amount of food. I count four varieties of gree vegetables in rectangular dishes, three types of potatoes – mashed boiled, and roast. She sits at the top of the table, Ryan facing, an I'm like an only child stuck in the middle.

She dishes casserole out onto three hot plates. I've no idea hov she handles them without mitts because I drop mine onto the ma when she hands it across.

'Jeez. It's hot.'

'Help yourself,' she says, ignoring me and poking a fork a the veg.

We toy with our food, each of us moving it with the speed o grand chess masters. Suddenly, Flo lifts a spoon, and bangs it o the table.

'Okay, guys. How's life been without me?'

'Sorry?' Ryan asks, as if he's misheard. If he was relaxed a moment ago, he's now sitting upright, his face draining of colour.

'It's a simple question. How has life been without me?' Flo looks from Ryan to me, and back again. She's surprisingly calm despite the clatter of spoon to get our attention.

I'm anything but calm, and Ryan looks as if an axe murderer has suddenly appeared. When neither of us says anything, Flo takes the lead.

'Let's eat up while you debate your answers. Go on. I've put in a lot of hard work.'

Flo stuffs a large forkful in her mouth.

Ryan sets his cutlery down.

'Not the same without you,' he says. 'That's what it's been like.'

'Ciara. Have you enjoyed your holiday?' Flo is now slicing through a rabbit thigh with a steak knife, and glaring at me in between cuts.

'I've had fun. Did a bit of sightseeing.'

'Did you look after Ryan?' Her eyes widen like saucers in the asking.

'I did a bit of cooking,' I say. 'Helped him load the washing machine.'

This back and forth goes on for a good five minutes, until Ryan finally breaks in.

'Ciara. When are you going back?' It's a brave opening gambit, and it's the first time his voice has risen above a whisper since I got here. Flo gets up, and drags her chair round the table to be close to Ryan. She takes his hand, links fingers.

'I haven't decided. It depends,' I say. You could hear a pin drop.

'I'm really sorry, Ciara. But now Flo's back, we're going to give our marriage another go.'

Flo takes both his hands now. She raises a questioning eyebrow at him, and I wonder if this is what she's told him, or his assumption.

'Is that what you want, Ryan? Really want?' I ask, and if looks could kill, Ryan would be dead meat. I glower at him, but he has no intention of coming clean.

Give him his due. He frees his hands from Flo's grip, and announces in a shaky voice, 'Yes, it is.'

I can almost hear him pray that I won't spoil the moment, that I'll play ball and help them honour their wedding vows.

'Perhaps you can stay at the pub? Or perhaps you'll head back to Ireland?' he asks.

Flo rolls her eyes, and takes back ownership of her husband's less than steady hands.

'I haven't decided what I'm going to do yet.' At least one of us is prepared to tell the truth.

It's like a bloody game of chess. Your move. My move. Her move.

Ryan then tries to divert the tension by telling Flo he'll tidy up, and apologises for not being hungry.

'Ryan. Are you going to tell her, or am I?' I blurt it out at the top of my voice.

'Tell me what?' Flo asks with nauseous measured calm. She then begins to round up the plates, slopping the leftover stew onto the one on top. There's so much left over that dollops splash onto the tablecloth.

'Ryan. Tell her!' I'm now yelling.

Ryan swivels his wedding band. He's seriously trying to hold himself in check when Flo chips in.

'Ciara. Why don't I answer for Ryan?' She plonks the dishes back down onto the table. 'It doesn't really matter what you want to tell me, or what you want Ryan to tell me. I can guess. But you know what? I'm here to stay, whatever. So, I suggest you go upstairs now, pack your bags, and get the hell out of our house.'

Despite the swearing, Flo is scarily self-controlled.

I scrape my chair back, and with a swipe, send my own glass smashing to the floor.

'I'll go. If that's what you both want.' I stare at Ryan, but he doesn't flinch. He really is going to take the easy option, and let Flo take the lead.

'Don't think you've seen the last of me. I'll get out of your hair now, but I'll be back.'

Ryan and Flo look at each other. He looks in shock, but she's grinning from ear to ear.

When she turns her back, Ryan gives me a wan smile. It's enough. Flo might have scored a minor victory, but I'm out to win the war.

70

FLO

Ryan suggests I follow Ciara upstairs.

'Make sure she doesn't take anything of yours.' He talks behind his hand, and I can hardly hear. But I'm pleased he doesn't trust her. 'I think she's been wearing some of your things.'

'I'm on it.'

I don't think Ryan recognised the Mint Velvet dress that Ciara is wearing, but I did. I might have a lot of clothes, but I've also got a great memory.

Ryan has no idea how shaken I am. I'm just about holding it together, yet I can't break down until she's gone. He looks worse than I feel, if that's possible. He hasn't moved from his seat, and I wonder if his legs are as wobbly as mine.

By the time I reach the spare bedroom, my anger bubbles up again. Ciara is facing the window, dressed in her underwear. The pants look crazily familiar, and I realise she's wearing my red bunny rabbit knickers.

Her case is almost full, and the zip halfway round. She must have bought a new suitcase because my pink tortoiseshell is in the corner. Ryan also suggested I check my jewellery boxes.

When I snooped earlier, I guessed it was the designer labels that had caught Ciara's eye. Now I'm not so sure. It's pretty freaky, but I think she's trying to look like me, and literally, step into my shoes. My clothes are certainly a snug fit. I know what she wore because YouTube taught me how to arrange clothes. There's an order to everything I own, and my system has been corrupted. But my bloody pants!

'Leave all my stuff behind,' I say. She nearly hits the ceiling. She's mortified at being caught in her underwear, doubly so because she's in my pants. She scrabbles round for a T-shirt.

'Glad you've taken off my dress. Did you think I wouldn't notice, or that I'd be happy to gift it in payment for having kept house?'

She whisks off the underpants and throws them on top of the laundry basket.

'Satisfied?' she asks, as she bends down, and retrieves a dirty pair from under the bed.

My passport, driving licence, jewellery, random clothes, and accessories are thrown on top of the duvet. I'll check everything before I let her leave.

I scuttle back down, and lock the front door. I'll rifle through her pockets before she goes, because, after tonight, I never want to see her again.

Ten minutes later, she's lugging her suitcase down the stairs, and Ryan has come out of hiding.

'I'll just check you haven't left anything behind,' I say. Translated, that you haven't stolen anything. I scoot back upstairs, and hear her trying to unlock the front door.

'Have you got the key?' she asks Ryan.

I suspect Ryan is looking back up the stairs. He won't have worked out that I pocketed the key, and as I can't hear any movement, I suspect he's sitting on the naughty step.

I go through all the rooms. Spare bedroom. Bathroom. An after a few deep breaths, I dare check the master bedroom.

Everything seems to be in its place. All my jewellery is there. wonder which pieces she wore? Maybe Ryan will tell me whe things get back to normal, whatever that's going to be.

Ryan looks like a little boy on the bottom stair, and he inche his shoulder aside to let me past. I wave the key.

'Is this what you're looking for?' I stab it in the lock, and ope the front door.

'Bye, Ciara.'

I nudge her suitcase down the steps, and only just pick u Ryan's muffled voice.

'Bye.'

'One more thing, Ciara. Don't ever come back,' I hiss, and slan the door after her.

Ryan creeps back into the kitchen, and grabs the wine bottle.

'Peace at last,' I say.

'It's so good to have you back, Flo. It's been hell.'

Not sure who has had it worse, but perhaps I'll never know. Al I do know is that it's a new beginning. There's a lot of work to do rebuilding trust, and getting to hear my husband's side of the story

Tomorrow I'll set to work. Now, I plan to get very drunk.

71

FLO

It's been a week since Ciara cleared out her stuff.

I'm assuming she's moved into the pub, lock, stock, and barrel, although there's the faint possibility she's gone back to Ireland. But I doubt it, and if I'm honest I'd rather have her close, at least until I know what she intends to do. She might disappear, but I doubt we'll be that lucky.

Ryan hasn't mentioned the video footage of him smothering his mother, although I've given him plenty of opportunity. I've been a good listener, encouraging him to tell me as much as he wants. He's unlikely to tell me everything, but I'll give him the chance. See how much he really trusts me, and how much he wants to make things work. In sickness and in health. I'm starting to suspect he has no idea of the evidence Ciara has, and am almost certain she never showed him. If Ryan finally gave in to his mother's pleas to help end it all, I think he'll tell me. Eventually.

Ryan is slipping quite easily back into contentment, and relief seems to follow him around. I waved him off for work, and the shoulder stoop has already straightened. There's an eerie normality about our daily routine, other than the fact that I'm sleeping in the spare room. Moving into the master bedroom is still a step too far.

'It's early days, Ryan,' I said. 'I'll need time.'

I pecked him on the cheek, and he didn't seem surprised when I deposited my bags on the spare bed. 'I'll sleep here. For now.'

'Of course. I totally understand. And again... I'm sorry, I'm sorry, I'm sorry. I love you.'

Tears drizzled down his cheeks as he stood in the doorway and watched me unpack.

He keeps apologising. I felt bad this morning when I snapped, reminding him I'm not his priest, and he doesn't need to spout Hail Marys for atonement. It's the Irish Catholic in him. He then apologised for apologising, and made me giggle, which didn't go down too well, but at least he's trying. And so am I.

I've been mooching about the house this morning, in private-detective mode, looking for clues. Evidence of I don't know what. Ciara's ghost follows me from room to room, and under the spare bed I pull out a recently used Tube ticket, and an empty packet of chewing gum. I wonder where she went in London. Did she go sightseeing? I can't quite smother the notion that she might have gone somewhere with Ryan.

She's been wearing my clothes. I know this because they're in random order, and I have to rearrange the hangers. My party clothes have had a thorough rummage. Patrick says he's told Ciara often enough to bin the tarty appearance, but rolls his eyes when he admits she enjoys wolf whistles as proof of her sexiness.

'No #MeToo concerns with Ciara. She laps it up,' Patrick said, having given up years ago trying to get her to tone it down.

When I've finished snooping, I close the door to the guest room, but leave the window wide to get rid of Ciara's lingering scent.

In the hall, I lift my Ted Baker coat off the peg. There's a black smudge near the collar, and I lick a finger and rub at it furiously. It won't budge, but expands and gets worse. I scrunch up the coat, take it through to the laundry room, and chuck it on top of the mountain of clothes. Everything Ciara touched will be going in the washing machine, or to the dry cleaner's. In the kitchen, I set to tackling the cupboards. I lift out plates, pots and pans, and upend the cutlery drawer, and start scrubbing the lot.

Ryan asked, before he left, if I'd be okay, as he's really worried about leaving me alone. As I straightened his tie, he asked if I had any plans.

'I'm going to do a late spring clean,' I announced.

'We can get a cleaner if you like,' he suggested.

When I used to insist I needed help around the house, Ryan would scoff. What else did I do all day?

'Maybe I should go away more often,' I said. It's hard not to milk the bonuses.

Ryan usually hates me being sarcastic, but today he circled my waist, and promised he'd be more than happy to pay for a cleaner.

When he confessed he should have done more housework when I wasn't around, I told him to go to work. Having him apologise for not using a duster. Really? There's only so much a girl wants to hear.

Adding the slovenly state of the house to his list of deadly sins took some bottle, even for Ryan.

A loud clank through the letter box makes me bang my head on a cupboard shelf. It's only the postman, but the slightest noises send me into a spin. As his feet crunch away across the gravel, I go to collect the post.

I pick up voices outside, and peek through the letter box, and see Olivia in her front path talking to the postman, gesticulating at the pile of junk mail he's given her. She's dressed like a washerwoman in a light blue buttoned-up nylon overall, and her hair is dragged so severely off her face that her wine-coloured birthmark under her ear is visible.

I open the door, and instantly Olivia looks over the postman's shoulder. She straightens up, and a hand shoots up to cover the birthmark. She's got a wide-eyed starey thing going on, but doesn't wave. She looks as if she's seen a ghost, and I'm sort of expecting her to scurry back inside, but she just stands and stares.

As the postman moseys off, I manage a weak smile. She's too far off to pick up it doesn't reach my eyes, but it should feed her confidence that perhaps I've mellowed.

'I don't want us to fall out,' she cried when she owned up to

aving had sex with Ryan. 'It was a stupid mistake, and was all my
ault.'

Actually, it was a two-way thing. Perhaps she'd have felt better
f I'd said as much. Instead I yelled until I was hoarse. She and
Ryan were equally to blame. It seems so long ago, but the hurt still
esters.

I step onto the porch, and hold my face up to the sun. When I
troll down the path, Olivia takes a tentative step forward, but
eeps her hands shoved in the baggy nylon pockets.

'Olivia,' I say. I sound like a policeman preparing to make an
rrest.

'Flo. How are you?'

I'm tempted to tell her the truth, but keep it simple. 'I'm fine
hanks. You?'

'We're both well.' Letting me know she's still with Kenneth is
avvy, even for Olivia.

She's looking at me, trying to weigh my mood. I know Olivia
well. Very well, actually. We spent hours together, drinking,
itching about the neighbours, and putting the world to rights. As
stand here, I remember her telling me how lucky I was to be
married to a man like Ryan.

'Kenneth is so bloody dull,' she'd said, comparing her
husband's blandness with Ryan's James Bond chiselled good looks.
thought it was big of her to say so, but that was before she came
close to destroying our marriage.

'Do you fancy a coffee? Or wine?' she asks. It's a daring ask.
Old times' sake?' Her voice wobbles.

'Why not. Let me go and lock up, and get my phone.'

'Great. I'll put the kettle on.' Her voice is suddenly chirpy, sing-
song with relief.

It seems to take forever to reach my own front door. Once

inside, I slam it, and collapse on the bottom stair, and count to ten. Then to twenty. Then all the way to one hundred.

I've been so engrossed with Ciara, her threats, fear of what she'll do next, that I haven't given Olivia much thought. Until now. Seeing her is bringing the nightmare back.

If Olivia hadn't slept with Ryan, I would never have left. I wouldn't have met Ciara, and Ryan I would still be okay. I could blame everything on Olivia.

I haul a brush through my hair, and pick up my phone. The sick feeling in my gut is getting worse, but I know I have to face Olivia. There are things I need to find out, and she's such a big mouth.

Their front door has been freshly painted a vile red, and it's wide when I stroll back across the street. There's no sign of Olivia but she's waiting for me.

'Yoo-hoo. I'm in the kitchen,' she yells.

It's as if I've never been away.

I must say Olivia's face is pastier, plumper than I remember. She's taken off her nylon overall, and it's hard not to stare at her thighs. Her jeans strain at the seams, she's put on so much weight. If I didn't know she couldn't have kids, I'd guess she was pregnant. She waddles like a duck in bare feet, her ankles swollen like melons.

'Thanks for coming,' she says with a shaky smile.

'Thought a catch-up would be good.' It's churlish not to thank her for asking me, but I'm not in the mood for overdoing the pleasantries.

I don't think Olivia is picking up the edge to my voice, as she nods towards *my stool*. It's one of a matching set of six red plastic stools that go up and down. Mine is nearest the window, at the far end of the central island. She beams when I sit down.

'When did you get back?' she asks.

She wraps a dishcloth round the screw top of a wine bottle, and sucks in her breath trying to find purchase. Before I've a chance to answer, she is arranging snacks on a revolving platter. Little glass dishes are slotted into a miniature lazy Susan which swivels as she piles it high with fattening snacks. Crisps. Doritos. Olives. Nuts, and stuffed peppers. The sight of Olivia's ballooning waistline makes me think she swivels the fancy platter when she's on her own.

'Just last week,' I say. 'Seems ages since I left,' I lie. Sitting on *my seat*, it feels like only yesterday.

She hands me a huge goblet of white wine, round which I have to wrap both hands.

'I only spotted you yesterday.' She swallows a large mouthful. 'Has Ciara left?'

She digs her fingers into the salt and vinegar crisps, and scoops out half of them.

'Oh, Ciara. She's gone. Did you meet her?' I know she did, Ryan told me.

But I'm here to listen. Olivia's two hobbies are eating, and gossiping. She rotates the lazy Susan, pointing a bitten nail at the stuffed peppers.

'Your favourites,' she says.

The sight makes me nauseous. I hold a palm up, shake my head.

'On a diet,' I say. She doesn't look taken aback, and loads her own plate higher.

'Yes. She came over when she arrived,' Olivia says.

'What did you think of her?' A sudden hiccup, and my hand wobbles, sending half my wine onto the floor. 'Shit. I'm really sorry.'

I'm not sorry at all, of course. The floor's sparkly, so it's pretty satisfying, and I need to avoid a fuzzy wine head.

'No worries. I'll wipe it up later.' She's more concerned to carry on the conversation, than to get cleaning. 'What did I think of her?' Olivia hums through a thin sliver of lips, as if considering. She's pretending that she didn't sum Ciara up in five minutes flat.

To give Olivia her due, she's a shrewd judge of character. She hasn't drunk enough to let rip, but she's bitchy about attractive women, and Ciara's not going to get away lightly.

'She seemed nice. She said you met in Bangor. That's where Ryan's mother lived?' She raises a questioning eyebrow.

'Yes. Ciara was a barmaid in Bangor.'

'Oh. She didn't tell me that.'

Why doesn't that surprise me?

My stomach knots, but my next question is the real reason why I'm here, and I've waited long enough.

73

FLO

'Did you see Ciara at the Hardens' garden party?'

'Yes, I did actually.' Olivia coughs up a peanut, catches it, and pops it back in her mouth. Her bulbous ankles pivot her stool, and the motion makes me feel I'm in a boat. 'She made quite an impression on the old men.'

Olivia lifts the wine from an ice bucket, and offers me a top-up. She's already pouring before I can nudge her hand away.

'No thanks. Watching my waistline,' I say, patting my stomach. Olivia doesn't pick up the dig, as she's preparing for full-blown gossip. 'Ryan told me she danced with everyone.'

I watch Olivia, reckoning if I don't blink, she'll back down, tell me all the gory details.

'Yes, she did indeed.' Olivia takes a deep breath. I've a desperate urge to clap my hands over my ears, and my gut is in full-churn mode. But if Ryan's and my marriage is going to stand a chance, I need to know everything. Even the gory details.

'I don't like to say, but...' Olivia sets down her glass. She's going to say it anyway. 'Ryan danced most of the night with Ciara. Pretty up close. I'm sorry.'

Bitch. It's not the telling, it's the pretending to be sorry that is the bitch part.

Olivia wears an expression somewhere between pity for me, and pride that she's told me. I can't help feeling that she's glad of the opportunity to paint Ryan as an incurable flirt. That he's always been the one to blame, even when he fucked her up against the garden fence.

'That's Ryan for you. A sucker for a pretty face, or even a not so pretty face.' I laugh. Again Olivia ignores the barb, but she's so drunk she mightn't have picked it up. Hopefully, she'll remember later.

I get up, push my glass aside.

'Thanks for the wine and nibbles. Like old times indeed.'

Before Olivia can extricate herself from the stool, which is stuck on its highest setting, I'm slopping across the wine I spilt on the floor. My pumps squelch all the way through to the hall.

By the front door, Olivia wedges herself between me and the frame.

'I'm really sorry, Flo. For what happened. Can you ever forgive me?' She sounds uncannily like Ryan. Two of a kind. I've counted five apologies since I got here.

'Already forgiven.' I stare at her. 'But I can't forget.'

She opens the door.

'Bye, Flo. And thanks.'

Her voice follows me down the path, across the road, up the path, and into the house. The door nearly flies off its hinges, as I slam it shut with both hands.